FINDING YOU

Elizabeth Holland

Thank you

Thank you to everyone that has contributed
towards the creation of this book.
A very special thank you to my wonderful beta readers.

CHAPTER ONE

Laura Harper

1st November 2020

The wind howled in the distance and Laura Harper pulled her sleeping bag tighter to ward off the icy gale. Only that morning the newspaper heading had warned that London was expecting a storm. The wind was bitter, and the cold stung her face as she tried to pull her woollen hat down to shield herself. Huddled in the doorway, Laura looked across the street to the flats above some shops. The warm glow of lights spilled out onto the dark street. Inside, Laura could see a living room. Perhaps there was a couple inside, huddled up on the sofa drinking hot chocolate and arguing about what series to watch next. Tears formed in Laura's eyes as she thought about how that should be her on this cold November night. It should have been her curled up on the sofa with Sean's arms around her. Instead, here she was lying on a damp cardboard box in a doorway. She had a second hand sleeping bag wrapped around her, desperately trying to keep the cold at bay and Sean... Sean was missing and presumed dead.

Laura felt herself trembling. She was unsure whether it was because of the cold, or her fear of being alone at night, in the midst of a terrible storm. A rumble of thunder filled her ears, and she jumped as her heart hammered in her chest. She took a deep breath, trying to calm herself. It didn't work. Instead, Laura undid her sleeping bag and shoved it into her backpack, which held her life's possessions. She couldn't stay here, she was too jumpy to stay in one place tonight. Laura could never stay in one place for too long, she was worried about being found. Who knew what *they* would do to her?

As the wind howled and the rain pelted down, Laura continued to walk through the backstreets of London. She passed many heaps of blankets with other homeless people huddled underneath them. By now, some of them would have consumed enough alcohol to have fallen into a state of unconsciousness. Sometimes, Laura wished she could do the same, but she knew it was too dangerous. She had to always be alert. As she passed under a bridge, Laura took a moment to stand and shelter from the rain. She was absolutely soaked. In the distance she could see Big Ben towering above the dark streets. She could just about make out the time. It was almost two in the morning. She would need to find somewhere to sleep soon. Before she knew it, rush hour would be upon her and she would have to find somewhere to hide herself until the crowds retreated. Once the morning rush hour ended, she could go in search of something to quell the hunger that was already gnawing away at her insides.

Laura made her way towards the underground and settled on making a bed for herself down one of the tunnels. There were a few other homeless people sleeping there, and so she felt somewhat safe. They might try to steal something from her, but that was the least of Laura's worries. Hopefully, these people would not try to kill her. With her sleeping bag wrapped around her again, Laura pushed her wet blonde hair back from her face. She was still cold and wet, but she would soon dry off with the luxury of a roof above her head.

As her eyes drifted shut, Laura thought about her friends and family back home. She hoped they were safe in their homes, not thinking about her. If her family or friends discovered where she was, then they would try to bring her home and Laura couldn't let them do that. While she was in London, living on the streets, everyone back at home in Manchester was safe. It was too risky for her to be around the people she loved. People were looking for her - dangerous people - and to an extent Laura was looking for them. She needed answers. She needed to know where Sean was and whether he was still alive. Over a year had passed since Laura had last seen Sean, but she had to keep searching for him, and for answers. It was only within the last few months that Laura began living on the streets, until then she had been staying in hostels.

29th August 2020,

Laura glanced down at the last few notes that she had hidden in her backpack. She could only afford a few more nights at a hostel and then she would be penniless. Before leaving Manchester, Laura had visited an ATM and withdrawn the maximum amount. The money had lasted her longer than she had expected, thanks to the cheap prices of the London hostels she had been staying in. Many of them were in the rough outskirts of London, but since losing Sean Laura had become fearless. She had suffered the worst pain imaginable, losing her beloved. Nobody could inflict more pain than that.

"Bathroom's free, Claire!" A young blonde woman called as she walked into the communal bedroom. Laura's head shot up at the sound of her false name. She had been going around under the name of Claire since the day she left Manchester. She couldn't risk anyone finding out her actual name or else it might get back to the wrong people and then they would know where she was.

"Thanks." She smiled back. The girl was a backpacker from Australia and they had been sharing a room for the last week. Their room held up to ten people, however only the two of them had stayed for more than one night, everyone else had moved on quickly. That suited Laura. Over the months Laura had got to know lots of travellers as they came and went from the various hostels - it had kept the loneliness at bay. However, nothing could stop the nightmares.

"I'll see you downstairs for breakfast," her new friend called after her as she took her towel to the bathroom.

After a rather cold shower in a communal bathroom, that had questionable levels of cleanliness, Laura emerged. She put her jogging bottoms and jumper back on. Over the months Laura's clothes were stolen or lost, as she never stayed in one place for too long. Laura tried to take her belongings wherever she went during the daytime, however sometimes it was impossible. She had visited various libraries and community centres trying to find information. However, all the news reports just listed Sean as missing. They hadn't even mentioned the suspicious circumstances. Laura knew that someone, somewhere, was trying to cover something up. She just hadn't discovered what that something was.

The breakfast room was almost empty by the time Laura entered. Her roommate was sitting at a table with a few people that Laura didn't recognise. Keeping her head down, Laura wandered over to the buffet table - which was a glorified trestle table with a few boxes of cereal on it - and poured herself some cornflakes and milk. Unable to think of an excuse, Laura took a seat with the other occupants and said a quick hello. She still kept her head lowered. Although she looked nothing like the Laura Harper that once lived in Manchester, she didn't want to take any unnecessary risks. The table continued their conversation about sightseeing whilst Laura's attention roamed the room. Her eyes fixated on the television on the wall behind her roommate's head. Laura's heart rate quickened as she recognised the picture being shown. It was Sean. Laura had seen the picture countless times, it was his official police portrait that hung in their hallway. A lump formed in her throat at the thought of their flat and the last memories she had inside those walls.

Laura strained her ears but the television's sound was muted, however somebody had switched the subtitles on, so Laura squinted her eyes to read them. Her breakfast churned in her stomach as she realised they were appealing for witnesses for both her and Sean. That was new, they had only previously mentioned Sean. However, the worse was yet to come. The screen flashed back to the news presenter who announced that Sean was presumed dead, however there had been some significant sightings of Laura. Laura took a deep breath to stifle the scream that was building within her - she had to get out of here and run. She couldn't risk being caught and being returned to her family, they would be in grave danger if she were.

Without saying a word, Laura slammed her spoon down and

ran to get her backpack. It was time she made the streets her home, she could fade into the shadows of London, whilst she tried to find the truth about what happened to Sean.

❖ ❖ ❖

CHAPTER TWO

Early the following morning, eager Londoners woke Laura as they marched through the underground tunnel. As they walked past, the smell of their coffee hit Laura's senses and her stomach grumbled with the thought of breakfast. The idea of walking into Pret a Manger and ordering a latte and a croissant filled Laura with joy. She could almost taste the sweet, buttery croissant as it would crumble in her hands before she could even get it to her mouth. The coffee would be strong and sweet, waking both her and her tastebuds. There would be no breakfast for Laura today, especially since she had no money left. Well, that wasn't strictly true. Laura had money in a bank account, however she had cut up her cards and thrown them away before making her way to London. If she used the cards, then the police could track her and the police would find her. She couldn't risk that, and so Laura had learned to beg for pennies and scraps of food. It was degrading and often fruitless, but it was life and it was what she had to do to survive.

After last night's storm, Laura emerged onto the street to see it strewn with fallen branches. There were some robust Londoners battling the gale force winds, some with their umbrellas blown inside out, others with their winter coats pulled tightly around them. All of them wore a miserable expression as they bowed their heads against the weather and forged on towards their destination. Laura knew from experience that a day like this would produce very little money or food. Everyone would be in too much of a hurry to notice her sat by the side of the road begging.

The day passed slowly as the hunger continued to gnaw away at Laura's insides. It had been an eventful morning with one particular commuter glaring down at her and telling her she should stop begging and get a job instead. If only they had known the story behind Laura's homelessness, Laura felt sure they would have acted differently. The anger in their eyes would have faded to pity as they skulked away, feeling guilty for making such assumptions. Instead of telling the commuter her story, Laura had held her head in embarrassment and hoped that they finished their rant quickly and moved along.

As the sun set above the Thames, Laura was yet to eat anything. She would have to visit one of the homeless shelters for dinner tonight. When possible, she tried to avoid the shelters in fear of someone recognising her from the television appeals that both her and Sean's family were conducting. The appeals had started back in August, whilst Laura was staying at a hostel. The police said fresh evidence had come to light, and they were appealing for the public's help in the disappearance of Laura Harper and the suspected murder of Sean Scott. Laura hoped they were wrong about Sean. She occasionally caught glimpses of the appeals as she walked past shops, and she knew they hadn't found a body... yet. It was only a matter of time before someone recognised her. She only hoped that someone would be one of the good guys. As the days passed, Laura grew more and more desperate for answers. Since leaving Manchester, Laura had lost a lot of weight and her signature blonde bob had grown out of control, now brushing the tops of her shoulder blades. Her haggard face no longer looked like the happy twenty-nine-year-old that she once was. With a sense of resignation, Laura packed up her belongings and began the short walk to the homeless shelter by Victoria Station. For a northern girl, she had quickly adjusted to the ways of London as she kept her head down and avoided making any eye contact on her short walk.

Eventually, Laura rounded the corner and came across the front door to the shelter. To her relief, the doors were open and she let herself in. The warmth enveloped her and the smell of food filled her nostrils. There was a gentle hum of conversation as Laura pushed open the door to the main hall where everyone sat eating and volunteers milled around trying to help and talk to the homeless. Keeping her head down, Laura walked towards the front counter and queued up for some food. Behind the counter stood a young man who looked around her own age, he was tall with thick black hair and dark green eyes that sparkled with concern.

"Good evening, what would you like?" he asked her as he pointed towards the array of food in front of him. Laura forced herself to concentrate on the food. Quickly, she pointed towards the curry. As soon as the mystery man had dished it up, she went to dash away.

"Would you like any cake?" he asked her, stopping her in her tracks. Laura turned back around to look at the cake on display. It was a lemon drizzle cake. Her mouth was watering just looking at it.

"I promise I didn't bake it." The man joked, he was already cutting Laura a slice after seeing the look on her face. "A woman named Isy occasionally drops off a cake on her way to work. Rumour has it she's about to upsticks and open her own cafe in Wales." Laura wasn't listening to what the man was saying, her focus was on how soothing the tone of his voice was. She took the cake from him. She would wrap it in a napkin and put it in her bag for tomorrow. Without uttering a word in reply, Laura took her tray and scurried away towards an empty table at the back of the room. She couldn't help the guilt that flooded her as she had almost lost herself in the stranger's compelling voice. His voice had been smooth and comforting, and Laura had felt herself falling under its spell. It was worlds apart from Sean's gruff tone, and Laura was annoyed at herself for appreciating a voice that was so different from the one that had once been her entire world. Grief tore at Laura's heart as she realised she might never hear Sean's voice again. The last few months had been particularly difficult and her thoughts were all over the place. Part of her wanted to give up, meanwhile the other part of her refused to give up until she discovered what had happened to Sean. It was a constant, exhausting battle with herself.

Trying to ignore the thoughts buzzing around her head and the stranger stood behind the food counter, who was still occasionally glancing her way, Laura turned her attention back to her food. As she took a bite of her curry, it surprised her how good it tasted. Her tastebuds sizzled as she picked out all the individual flavours; turmeric, cumin seeds, black mustard seeds, and a hint of aniseed. It surprised Laura how quickly she had identified the flavours. Her life as a chef was a lifetime ago, but all of those years of training would never leave her. Despite this, there was something else in the dish, a flavour that she didn't recognise. As she continued to eat her first meal of the day, Laura saw the shadow of someone sit down opposite her. A knot formed in her stomach and she completely lost her appetite. *They* had found her. Would she have enough time to run?

Time stood still as Laura looked up from her meal, keeping her knife and fork in her hands. They could be used as a weapon if she had to. She'd worked in kitchens long enough to know that these everyday objects could do a lot of damage. With her heart hammering in her chest and a sick feeling in the pit of her stomach, Laura slowly looked up to see who had sat down. She sighed in relief as she realised that the man sat opposite her was the same one that had just served her dinner. Her grip on the cutlery loosened, and the tension left her body.

"Sorry, I didn't mean to startle you." His voice was deep, but he seemed unsure of himself, like he didn't really know what to say to her.

"It's okay." Laura's voice came out as a whisper as she focused on her breathing to stop the panic attack that had been about to burst out of her. Every inch of her body was screaming at her to run. It had been so long since someone had sat close to her, and talked to her, that it felt wrong. She forced herself to relax, it was only one of the helpers at the shelter, he wouldn't harm her.

"We're encouraged to sit with people and talk to them. Sorry, it's my first night here, so I'm not sure what to say." The man ran his hand through his dark hair as he shot

Laura a nervous smile.

"You don't have to talk to me." Laura shrugged her shoulders and looked down at the half eaten food in front of her. She had grown unaccustomed to making eye contact with people.

"Why don't we start by introducing ourselves? I'm Luke." Ignoring Laura's stand-offish attitude, Luke stretched his hand across the table for Laura to shake. With a sigh, Laura took his hand and gave it a brief shake. His touch was soft and there was something reassuring in the way his hand held hers. For a moment she felt safe. Laura shook her head to clear the thought from her mind. She couldn't allow herself to feel safe. If she thought she was safe, she would be vulnerable.

"I'm Claire." The lie slid effortlessly off of her tongue.

"Lovely to meet you, Claire. Can we do anything for you, other than a hot meal?" Laura rolled her eyes at Luke's words. He sounded as though he was reading from a script. She just wanted to eat her dinner in peace and then skulk off into the night to find somewhere safe, and hopefully dry, to sleep.

"No, thank you." She shrugged her shoulders and turned her attention back to the half eaten plate of food, hoping he would get the hint and leave her alone. He didn't.

"Perhaps we could help you get back in touch with your family?" Laura knew he meant well, but she really just wanted him to leave her alone. At the mention of her family, her eyes filled with tears, there was nothing she wanted more than a hug from her mum, a reassuring nod from her father, and a badly timed joke from her younger brother. She missed her family so much, but she knew she had to stay away from them to keep them safe.

"Claire?" Laura's head jerked up at the sound of her false name, she had almost forgotten that Luke was sitting opposite her. By now, her food had gone cold, and all she wanted was to leave for the night and find somewhere safe to sleep. Her eyes were drooping, and she was struggling to focus on the conversation. There was a glint in Luke's eyes that unnerved Laura - why was he so eager to speak to her? Laura shook her head to rid herself of the thought. She was just tired and suspicious of everyone. That was just who she was these days.

"Sorry, I've just got a lot on my mind. Thank you for trying to help but I have to go." Laura grabbed her bag as Luke was distracted by shouting on the other side of the room, she surreptitiously put the knife she had been using in her bag - It didn't hurt to have some form of protection on her. Other shelter staff had calmed the man down and Luke's attentions returned to her.

"Well, you know where we are Claire, please come back, and have a think about how we might help you. I'll see you soon!" Luke's face lit up, and he flashed her a smile. A spark flowed through her. Immediately, guilt enveloped her. How could she be admiring another man's smile when Sean was missing and presumed dead? Especially the smile of a man who she didn't even trust.

Without saying another word, Laura ran from the room, ignoring all the eyes that turned on her as she rushed to make her way to the door. Thankfully, she was soon through the door and breathing in the fresh air. She knew Luke was only doing his job and being kind, but it was her reaction to him that had upset her. How could she be thinking about another man after everything that had happened? With a sigh, Laura pulled her hood up to cover her face and made her way over towards the shadows. A strange tiredness had come over her and she was finding it difficult to focus. Laura knew she had to find somewhere to sleep.

She finally settled down under a bridge, along a canal. She knew it would be quiet, and there was little chance of anyone, besides other homeless people, coming across her. Laura hugged her bag close to herself as her heavy eyes closed. As her consciousness slipped from her, she was comforted knowing that she had a knife stashed away in the side pocket of her bag. She would have to be careful for the next couple of days now that she had shown her face somewhere.

CHAPTER THREE

As the sun rose in the sky and the birds started chirping, Laura woke. During her time on the streets, she had learned how to sleep lightly. As soon as her eyes were open, she was alert. Today, however, everything was a little harder. Her body was slow, each slight movement was a monumental task, and her mind was slow and foggy. It was almost like she was suffering from a hangover. Despite this, she packed up her belongings and readied herself for another tiresome day of begging for food and money. Laura was cold and would have loved a shower, but she knew it was too risky to visit another shelter so soon after last night. She would have to keep a low profile for a while and check newspapers to see if anyone had recognised her.

Once Laura had packed up and was back on the streets looking for food, she couldn't shake the image of Luke from her head. He had been so kind and considerate, and he had genuinely seemed to want to help her. Laura couldn't deny the fact that he was also very good looking, and he had eyes she could get lost in, if she wasn't so jumpy and alert all the time. For a moment, Laura allowed her imagination to run away with itself as she thought about what it might be like to live with Luke - to wake up next to him every day and to feel safe walking around the streets of London with him by her side. As

Laura lost herself in the thought, pain coursed through her body. How could she be thinking about Luke? What about Sean? Laura mentally chastised herself. She couldn't allow someone to lure her into trusting them just because they were nice to her. Thankfully, she would never have to see Luke again.

Laura pushed her way through the London crowds and allowed the pain of Sean's loss to pierce through the protective wall she had built. She needed to feel the pain, to remind herself just how much she missed him. To remind herself why she was living on the streets and searching for answers. Today, she would visit Waterloo library to use their computers. Laura had exhausted every avenue of research, however that didn't mean she could just give up. She had to find out what happened to Sean. What if he was still alive? Laura thought back to the night she realised Sean was missing. With the pain came the memories of a day that Laura would never forget.

27th October 2019,

Laura breathed a sigh of relief as she plated up the last meal of the day. Her shift was finally over and she could rest her feet for the first time in hours. As she pulled her chef's hat off and unbuttoned her jacket, she revelled in the cool air that hit her. It had been so hot and stuffy in the kitchen. It was Laura's night off, however her colleague, Paul, had called in sick, meaning that she had to step in at the last minute and cover for him. She had planned a quiet night in with wine and a takeaway with her boyfriend, Sean. Instead, she had been toiling away in a hot kitchen all night.

The kitchen team had said they would clear up without Laura's help tonight, and so she shouted her goodbye and ran out to her car. She hoped she might still get an hour tonight with Sean. They had barely seen each other lately, what with her working in the kitchen so often, and he had been busy at work. Unfortunately, a police officer's job was never complete. Tonight had been the first night in weeks that both their schedules were free, and yet they still hadn't spent any time together. Laura sent Sean a quick text telling him she was on her way home and that she had also grabbed a leftover slice of apple pie to bring home with her, his favourite dessert.

As Laura pulled up outside the flat she shared with Sean, a funny feeling settled in the pit of her stomach. Something seemed off. Dismissing the feeling, Laura scooped up her belongings, balancing the apple pie on the top, before making her way towards the block of flats. Thankfully, someone was just coming out and so they held the door open for her. Laura made her way up the two flights of stairs and along the hallway to flat number Twelve. The uneasiness resurfaced and she found herself unable to dismiss it.

The door to their flat was open slightly, however that was not unusual. She often got home with armfuls of clothes and food, and so Sean would leave the door on the latch for her to just push it open. That evening she did just that, calling out a hello as she closed the door behind her. She was met with silence. Laura dumped all the items in her arms on the console table in the hallway and made her way into the living room to see what Sean was doing.

Laura pushed open the living room door and before she could stop herself, she screamed. It was a sound she had never heard herself make before. With trembling hands, she ran back to the front door and opened it. Once out on the landing, uncontrollable sobs ripped through her body. Her neighbours all came rushing out to see what the commotion was but Laura couldn't form any words, all she could do was scream in-between sobs and point towards her front door.

The scene she had walked in on would haunt her forever. Their usually tidy living room was a mess with the furniture overturned - every surface cleared of its contents. Drawers had been flung open, and the contents were lying in piles on the floor. However, that hadn't been what had made Laura scream. In the middle of the room, just behind their upturned sofa, was an enormous pool of blood. Next to it was Sean's wallet and phone. Laura had fled the flat, terrified of what she might see next or who might still be in there. As the neighbours flocked around her, she tried to form sentences.

"Sean. Where's Sean?" Laura gasped out in between sobs. "Sean could be lying somewhere in the flat, bleeding to death. Has someone called an ambulance?" This time Laura's voice came out loud and clear. She was shouting. She felt for her phone in her pockets before realising that it was on the pile of items she had left on the console table. With another scream of anguish she threw herself towards the door, trying to get through to get her phone.

"Laura, calm down, please. Sean's not in there." Simon, their neighbour, put a hand on Laura's shoulder to calm her. He had been the first person to come to Laura's aid and had run straight into the flat to see what the matter was.

"What do you mean he's not in there?" If he wasn't in there, then where was he?

Adrenaline took over, and Laura could think with some clar-

ity. Perhaps he had been hurt, but with his police training he had probably taken himself to hospital. She took a breath to calm herself. If she could just get to her phone, she could call Sean's parents. The hospital would have called Sean's next of kin, and since they weren't married, that would have been his parents. They would know where he was.

"The police are here." Simon announced. Laura took a deep breath to collect her thoughts. The police could call the hospital and find out how Sean was. She hoped it might be one of his colleagues.

As the officers stepped out of the lift, Laura was disappointed as she didn't recognise either of them. The two men strolled over towards the entrance of the flat where Laura was standing, with Simon by her side.

"Miss Harper?" One officer asked, the other remained silent, staring down at his shoes.

"Yes. My boyfriend, Sean Scott, has gone missing and there's blood covering our living room." Laura's voice wobbled as she spoke, but she controlled her emotions for long enough to explain the situation to the officers.

"Miss Harper, my name is Logan. There will be other officers along shortly to review the crime scene, however we're here to ensure your safety. We'd like you to come with us, please." The same man spoke, whilst the other kept staring down at his shoes. Perhaps he was new to the job. Laura was terrified. They had sent officers to keep her safe before they even looked at the crime scene. She knew enough about Sean's day-to-day work life to know that this was not the normal procedure. The situation must be serious.

"Where are we going?" Laura asked.

"We'll take you to the hospital to see Sean and then from there we will take you to a safe house." The promise of seeing Sean was all that Laura needed to hear. She didn't even think to pick up her phone or her bag. Thankfully, she had stopped for petrol on her way home so her bank card was in her pocket. She said her thanks to Simon and followed the officers back down to their car. They led Laura to a plain car parked across the road. Both men kept looking around them to ensure there was nobody around. Laura knew she should be scared, her life was in danger, however all she could think about was seeing Sean.

She climbed into the back of the car and put her seat belt on as both officers climbed in the front. Nobody said a word as they drove through the city. It wasn't until they got to a crossroads that fear set in. They had driven straight over, but to get to the hospital you had to turn left. Laura was sure there wasn't another route. With sudden clarity, she replayed the events in her head. When the officers arrived, neither of them had shown a badge. This was something Sean had always warned her about. They had seemed jumpy, but Laura had put it down to the dangerous situation. But what if that wasn't the reason? She had been too concerned for Sean's safety to even consider her own.

The car doors were unlocked, and so Laura knew she could escape.

"What station did you say you're from?" she asked, trying to hide the tremble in her voice. The same officer that had done all the talking responded. They were from the same station as Sean. An icy chill ran down Laura's spine. Sean always spoke to her about work and would tell her when they had any new recruits, not once had he ever mentioned these two officers. Logan was a distinctive name and Laura would have remem-

bered it. The other officer was clearly new and young, and yet Sean had not mentioned any new recruits in a long while. She was almost certain that these men were lying to her.

The car slowed at another set of traffic lights, and Laura knew that this was her only opportunity to run. Silently, she undid her seatbelt, ensuring that neither of the men in front noticed. Without thinking too much, she threw open the car door and ran. She heard the heavy footsteps as they ran after her. Both men were shouting at her, angry and threatening.

"Come back!" The officer named Logan shouted after her. A sob rose in Laura's chest and she knew she couldn't prevent it, however she had to keep running. So that's what she did. She ran, and she ran until there was no way they could still be following her.

The sound of a car horn pulled Laura from her memories. It took a moment for her to focus on the events surrounding her. She was still in London, however she had been walking blindly through the streets as she relived the events of that night. Laura turned her head in search of the noise when her eyes settled on a familiar face. It was Luke from the shelter. Another beep made her jump, and she turned towards it. It was too late though, inches away from her was a bus. Laura whipped her head back to the spot where Luke had been standing, but he wasn't there anymore. She must have imagined it. The sound of the brakes squealed throughout Laura's ears and the smell of burnt rubber from the tyres filled her nostrils. Before she could react and jump out of the way, the bus hit her. The searing pain ripped through Laura's body. She couldn't scream, she couldn't do anything. She could feel her consciousness slipping, she didn't fight it. Perhaps now she could reunite with Sean.

"Move out the way, I'm a doctor!" was the last thing Laura heard before she allowed the darkness to steal away her consciousness.

CHAPTER FOUR

The first thing Laura was aware of was the pain. A hot, harrowing pain that was consuming her entire body. She didn't know whether to fight it or to allow it to take hold of her. Was this what death felt like? Laura hoped Sean hadn't experienced this kind of pain on that fateful night. Despite the searing pain, the thought of Sean going through this hurt her even more. It was a different type of pain, this one manifested in her heart and tore through to her soul. She couldn't bear to think about what he might have gone through.

"Hello?" There was a voice calling to Laura, it sounded far away. She recognised the voice and for a moment Laura wondered whether it was Sean's. As her senses returned to her, she realised it wasn't Sean's voice she was hearing, it was Luke's. Fear filled Laura's body. Why was she with Luke? Had he been following her ever since their encounter that morning? There had been something about him at the shelter that made her doubt his authenticity. Was he working for *them?*

Laura fought with her body to regain consciousness. She needed to run. Although, how she would run whilst battling this pain, she did not know. The pain coursing through her body hadn't eased in the slightest. As she successfully prized open her eyes, a bright light blinded her. Slowly, she blinked and focused on the room surrounding her. She was in a hospital room. Laura took a deep breath to steady herself and tried to piece together what was happening. Standing around her bed were three people, Luke and two friendly looking nurses, one male and one female. They were all staring at her as though they were waiting for her to do something entertaining. Laura stared in disbelief at the sight of Luke standing at the end of her bed. What was he doing here?

Ignoring her audience, Laura focused her attention on herself. She was lying in a hospital bed and as she looked around at her body; she discovered her right leg was in plaster and she had big purple bruises on her left arm. Laura winced as she tried to sit up. She must have broken some ribs.

"What happened?" she eventually stuttered out. Her mouth was incredibly dry and she struggled to unstick her tongue from the roof of her mouth.

"Good afternoon, Claire. I'm Doctor Bell and I'll be looking after you during your stay at Guy's Hospital." Luke beamed at her and walked around to the side of the bed. For a second, Laura felt confused why he was calling her Claire, however her senses quickly caught up with her.

"What happened?" she asked again. Her fear retreated slightly as she realised he was still under the impression that her name was Claire. Perhaps it was a coincidence that he was her doctor.

"You don't remember?" Luke's voice pulled Laura from her musing. His brow knitted into a frown.

"No." Laura shook her head. Why didn't she remember? More importantly, what didn't she remember?

"It's okay," Luke reassured her as he saw the fear cross her face, "you hit your head so it's probably the concussion that's made you forget. Why don't we start with some basic questions? What's your full name and address?" He smiled at her as he took a seat next to her bed, waiting for her response. Laura didn't know what to do or say. She knew who she was, but she couldn't tell him - she could not tell anyone. She would have to lie and hope he didn't check her details. If he did, she would either be in big trouble or they would think she had lost her memory completely. Laura took a deep breath to steady her nerves. So much for starting with basic questions.

"My name is Claire Smith, and I don't have a permanent address at the moment." Laura could only hope that there were many more Claire Smiths out there.

"Of course, sorry. I shouldn't have asked about your address. I think we have confirmed that there's no real memory loss. How are you feeling?"

"I feel like I've been hit by a bus." Laura winced as she tried to sit up in bed, her ribs were protesting.

"Funny you should say that. You were, in fact, hit by a bus." As the words came tumbling out of Luke's mouth, Laura had a sudden flash of memory. She had been blindly walking along the streets of London thinking about Sean. She must have walked into the road without realising. Memories suddenly flooded back to her. She was sure she had seen him before the bus hit her. However, her mind had been playing tricks on her. It always happened when she thought about Sean, the trauma would confuse her brain.

"Claire, I'm sorry, but I have to ask this and these two nurses have to witness your answer. Was this an accident or were you attempting to take your own life?"

Laura's head was spinning as she thought about the question. She hadn't meant to walk in front of the bus, but perhaps she had subconsciously wanted all the pain to end. Well, that hadn't worked in her favour. Now she was in a hospital bed in even more pain.

"It was an accident." Whether she meant to kill herself, she couldn't have these people thinking she was suicidal. If they did, then they wouldn't let her out of their sight.

"Good. Now, I'm going to talk you through your injuries. It will sound worse than it is, I promise." Despite the fear welling up inside, Laura still felt butterflies in her stomach as Luke shot her a reassuring smile.

"You have broken your ankle, thankfully it's a clean break and should heal on its own, but you will be in a cast for a while. You have also broken three ribs, which pierced your lung. We've patched you up, but you will be in some pain whilst they heal. As you have already discovered, you also suffered some concussion. You'll probably have some general pains and bruising, but overall I think you got off rather lightly after being hit by a bus." Despite being the bearer of bad news, Luke kept his reassuring smile plastered across his face the entire time. Laura was trying to keep calm as she considered all of her injuries, she would be in a lot of pain for a while now. How was she going to sleep rough with all these broken bones?

"How long will I have to stay here for?" asked Laura.

She wasn't sure she wanted to know the answer. Despite being fearful of someone discovering her true identity, it was nice to be lying in an actual bed and to know that they would feed her throughout the day.

"Let's see how your body reacts and how quickly you heal. I know your situation, Claire, we will not be discharging you back onto the streets anytime soon. I have more patients to see, but I'll pop back and see how you're doing once I have finished my rounds." He gave her one last dazzling smile and left the room with the two nurses following behind him, both of whom had told her to get some rest.

Laura knew there was no point lying there and dwelling on what had happened, and so she took their advice and rested. Who knew the next time she would get to sleep in a bed?

CHAPTER FIVE

Laura was unsure how long she had been asleep for, but when she woke she was aware of someone else's presence in the room. She smiled sleepily to herself as she thought about how she would open her eyes to see Luke's gorgeous green eyes staring back at her. Laura fought through the fog to pry open her sleepy eyes, wanting to say thank you to Luke for being so caring and for reassuring her. She had been wrong to judge him so quickly when he was just trying to help her. As the glaring light flooded her senses, it took Laura a few seconds to adjust to the brightly lit room. However, as she took in her surroundings, it soon became apparent that it was not Luke in the room with her. Every nerve within Laura's body was tingling, her brain was screaming at her to run, but she was paralysed with fear. Perhaps this was it, this was the end. Being hit by a bus had been a complete waste of time because this was how she was going to die.

There were two men in her hospital room, both wearing black jeans and black biker jackets. She suspected it was a uniform so that they could not be easily identified. Sean had taught her that. During his time as a police officer, he had come across lots of organised crime groups that would adopt a 'uniform'. What if these two men were the last people Sean had seen? Laura's head pounded with anger as she considered the pain that these two men could have inflicted on him. The kindest man you could ever meet and yet these monsters had subjected him to such pain and horror, leaving behind just a puddle of blood.

"Good afternoon, Laura." The man almost spat her name as he strolled closer to the hospital bed. The second man was on the other side of her bed, looking at all the machines that were monitoring her and administering morphine for her pain. Laura only hoped that they wouldn't be able to fiddle with them and give her an overdose. As much as she wanted to be with Sean, she didn't want it to be like this. They wouldn't have the satisfaction of taking her life too.

"What do you want?" Laura's voice was still raspy from sleep, preventing her from conveying the anger that was bubbling away inside her. She was scared and vulnerable, and there was no way of hiding it with her leg in a cast and hundreds of wires attached to her. Not to mention the stupid heart rate monitor that was not-so-quietly telling everyone just how scared she was.

The man smirked at her, showing a row of rotten teeth. Oversized black sunglasses hid his face, they were the same as the ones the second man was wearing. Both men had beards, they were another aspect of the uniform. Between their glasses and beards, there was very little that would distinguish them. Laura knew from all the discussions she'd had with Sean about his work that this was an organised crime group, they knew what they were doing.

"We want you and everything you know." The man spat at her. She recoiled from the stench that was emitting from his rotting mouth.

"I don't know anything." Laura tried to sound brave, but her voice was a mere squeak. She was feeling far from brave at this moment in time. She was all too aware how easily the men could tamper with her morphine and kill her.

"Well, we think you know everything. Sean definitely did, he just needed a bit of encouragement before he spoke." The smug look on the man's face made Laura feel sick. How dare they talk about Sean like that?

Courage welled up inside of Laura. She knew she had to call for help or else she would be dead in the next few minutes. They had already harmed and possibly killed Sean. They wouldn't think twice about ending her life. She took a deep breath to fill her lungs with air and at the top of her lungs she screamed out, "Help!". One man gripped her bad leg, sending pain shooting through her body. She immediately stopped shouting and instead whimpered in pain. Meanwhile, the other man pulled a pillow from underneath her and pressed it to her face, muffling her cries of agony, whilst also cutting off her supply of oxygen.

Panic flooded Laura as she realised she couldn't breathe. This was it, they were killing her.

As Laura's survival instinct kicked in and she tried to push the pillow from her face, she heard a door open and the sound of someone shouting. Suddenly, the pressure on top of the pillow disappeared and Laura took a few deep breaths before pushing it from her face. She took in the scene in front of her, Luke was sprawled out on the ground. Meanwhile, both of the men were leaping over him and running for the door.

"Stop! Security!" shouted Luke as he scrambled to stand up. The hospital floor was slippery, meaning that the two men had just enough time to run before Luke could alert anyone. Instead of running after them, he approached Laura's bed.

"Are you okay?" he asked, checking the machines ensuring nobody had tampered with them.

"I think so." Laura stuttered out, still in shock over what had just happened. She'd just been face to face with people connected to Sean's murder. She wished she had been smart enough to come up with a plan to catch them or at the very least hurt them. It was too late now though, at least she was still alive. Laura was angry and frustrated. That was the closest she had been to any answers for over a year, and yet she still didn't know why these men were trying to kill her.

"What happened?" he asked as he took a seat next to her bed, concern etched across his face.

Laura was speechless for a few moments, unsure just how much she should tell Luke. After all, he was a stranger. However, her brain could not come up with a plausible lie and he had seen too much for her to just brush it off. She had to trust him, after all, he had saved her life.

"They've been after me for a while, it's why I've been living rough." She was embarrassed to say it out loud. She had allowed someone to scare her so much that she could not go home.

"Who are they?" he asked her, leaning forward and taking

hold of her hand. Laura knew it was wrong in the circumstances, but she couldn't help the brief smile that formed on her face as his soft hand protectively held hers.

"I don't know. All I know is they killed my boyfriend." A silence hung in the air after Laura's revelation. She did not want to go into detail about Sean being missing and presumed dead. If she did, then Luke could search the case online. It was easier to say that Sean was dead. Luke squeezed her hand, but he didn't know what to say. Few people knew what to say after you told them your boyfriend was brutally murdered. Even after experiencing it firsthand, Laura wouldn't know what to say to someone in her position. Nothing you could say could make it better or take away the pain, and so it was one of those occasions where words were better left unsaid.

"Do you not have family who can look after you?" Luke asked her. He was still holding her hand.

"I don't want to put them in any danger." Laura knew that if she contacted her family, they would have her home in an instant. They wouldn't worry if they were putting themselves in danger. They loved her and wanted her to be safe. However, she felt the same about them and that was why she had to stay away. The men would find her at home, and then her family would be in danger.

"Claire, you can't sleep rough on the streets with a broken ankle. I'm not supposed to do this so please don't tell anyone I've offered, but I'd like you to come and stay with me." Laura opened her mouth to protest but Luke cut her off. "Claire, I insist. How on earth would you even get up and down from the ground with your leg in a cast?" Laura bit back the retort that she had already planned

- she had intended to sleep on park benches. Could she really stay with Luke? If she could get out of the hospital unseen, then nobody would know she was there, and nobody would make a connection between her and the handsome doctor. He had proven to her she could trust him, so what did she have to lose?

"Are you sure?" Laura asked. She couldn't deny that the prospect of getting to sleep in a proper bed for a little longer and having access to food and a bathroom excited her.

"I'm sure. I have other people to see, but I'm going to get a security guard to stand outside your room to ensure those men do not come back."

As soon as Luke left the room, the smile that she had plastered across her face disappeared. Now that he was no longer sat beside her and holding her hand, the reality of what had just happened hit her. They had found her. How had they found her? She had been going under a false name and so they couldn't have traced her through any hospital records. Someone must have been following her the whole time, just waiting for a moment where she was vulnerable. A shiver ran down her spine at the thought. Was it not enough that she had lost Sean, the love of her life? She had experienced so much trauma and yet here she was still trying to get through each day. She didn't know why, though. Without Sean, she had no future. Guilt seeped in as Laura realised she was picturing Luke's friendly face. Did she really have no future? She shook her head to dispel the thoughts. She had to focus on finding answers or else she would continue running away from a danger she did not truly understand.

CHAPTER SIX

The following day, Luke discharged Laura and left her in the hospital cafeteria sipping a rather vile polystyrene cup of coffee whilst he finished his shift. She was wearing a baseball cap to keep her identity hidden, and Luke had asked the security guards to keep an eye on her. Laura couldn't complain, there were lots of people around and so she was somewhat safe; she was also under the influence of a large dose of morphine, and so she was happy to just sit back and watch the world pass her by. She watched as elderly couples wandered past, hand in hand. Some had smiles on their faces after receiving good news, others looked as though they had been dabbing tears from their eyes. An endless stream of children ran past, followed by a few in wheelchairs. As each person passed, Laura wondered what their story was. Nobody would look at her and guess how much she had suffered, and so it made her wonder what was going on in other peoples' lives.

As Laura continued to watch the couples wandering through the hospital's maze of corridors, a wave of emotion crashed over her. She had been forced to be brave and to run to protect herself, but in doing so she had never had the chance to process everything that had happened. She didn't even know whether they had found Sean's body while she was in hospital - perhaps she had even missed his funeral. They were thoughts she couldn't entertain, and so instead, Laura turned her attention to one of the discarded newspapers on the table in front of her. She ignored the news sections and skipped straight to the celebrity gossip. There was enough drama going on in her own life, she didn't need to hear about how many local stabbings there had been in the last twenty-four hours.

After what seemed like hours, but was probably only half an hour, Luke walked over to her and helped her up from her seat. Luke took her bag from her and passed her some crutches, telling her she would get used to them.

"Do you have a car?" she asked, a sudden realisation hit her she might have to get on public transport. Laura suspected that would not end well, she would probably come out of it with two legs in casts.

"No, I don't, but don't worry, I don't expect you to jump on the tube. I thought we would get a taxi." Luke had thought it through, much to Laura's relief, and so she hobbled along after him, still trying to coordinate walking with crutches.

Once outside the hospital, Luke effortlessly hailed them a taxi, and he helped her inside. He gave the driver his address, and they both settled back into their seats to enjoy their journey through rush-hour London. Laura kept sneaking sly glances towards Luke. Even in the artificial light shining down from office blocks and takeaway shops, he looked good. His inquisitive eyes shone as he looked down at his phone. How did he look so good after doing a twelve-hour shift? Laura admired the stranger sat next to her, he was so kind, dedicating his life to helping others.

"Do you live far away?" Laura asked him. She was now feeling excited about her stay with the handsome doctor. She needed to stop her thoughts from straying to how lovely he was to look at. The morphine in her system wasn't helping the situation.

"I live near London Bridge." He smiled at her before turning back to the messages on his phone. Feeling a little disheartened, Laura decided not to disturb him again, instead she turned her attention to the window. She watched as the night sky drew in and the bright lights of London twinkled around her. She had been to London Bridge once before, with Sean.

◆ ◆ ◆

1st June 2016,

They had visited London to celebrate their eight-year anniversary. Sean had booked it as a surprise and had even arranged her time off work. On the Friday morning, he had woken her up with breakfast in bed, and told her to pack because they had a train to catch in a couple of hours. Sean kept their destination a secret until they arrived at the train station and she spotted the train they were getting. It read London Bridge.

"London? We're going to London?" She squealed, she was bubbling over with excitement at the thought of her and Sean visiting the bright lights of London. Neither of them had ever been before, but both had talked about going one day.

"Are you happy?" Sean asked, taking her suitcase from her so she could board the train safely.

"I'm beyond happy."

They chose their seats, and Laura didn't stop talking the entire journey. She discovered Sean had booked a hotel, theatre performances and knowing her love of food he had carefully booked a different restaurant each night. He had planned it all to perfection - even making no plans on their first night so they could explore.

The weekend had been a whirlwind of excitement as they explored, went to the theatre and ate tons of delicious food. It was the happiest Laura had ever been, and she fell even more in love with Sean. The first night had been heavenly.

"Where shall we eat?" Laura asked as she finished touching up her makeup. The hotel room was breathtaking. As they had walked into the room, Laura's eyes had immediately been drawn to the four-poster bed, in the centre of the room, adorned with luxurious gold silk bedding. The room itself was stunning, with floor to ceiling windows overlooking Hyde Park. Sean had done very well.

"I thought we could just take a walk and see where we end up?" He strolled over to where she sat at the vanity table and placed a kiss on the top of her head.

"Sounds perfect." She beamed back at him.

Together, they had walked hand in hand around London, taking in the twinkling lights and the jolly atmosphere. Eventually, they came across a little bar near Covent Garden, nestled along a busy street. Inside, the bar was dimly lit with candles on each table. They sat in that little bar for hours, drinking copious amounts of gin and gorging on Tapas.

"I wish every day could be like this." Laura sighed. Sean's eyes

glimmered in the candlelight as he reached across the table to take her hand in his.

"Perhaps one day it could be. There's nothing stopping us from going anywhere in the world. You can cook and I can entertain. We could have our own little bar like this."

Laura smiled serenely in her drunken haze as she considered cooking in her own kitchen, setting her own hours, and her own menu. That was the ultimate dream.

"One day." She squeezed Sean's hand and gazed into his eyes. There was nowhere else in the world she would rather be.

The entire trip had been wonderful. It had been absolute perfection as they walked hand in hand along the Thames with the night sky above them, stopping now and then to take in the world around them. The stars twinkled as they discussed their future plans of owning a romantic bar on the edge of a Spanish beach.

◆ ◆ ◆

"Claire, are you okay?" A voice pulled Laura from her thoughts and she angrily swiped away at the tears that were running down her cheeks. She had to stop thinking about Sean. He was gone, and their perfect future, that they had planned together, was no longer a possibility. She had tried searching for him, but that had ended in her almost being killed.

"Sorry, Luke, what did you say? I was a million miles away." Plastering a smile on her face, Laura turned to face him. She couldn't help but notice the differences in his and Sean's appearance. Sean's eyes were blue, whilst Luke's were green. Their hair was different shades, and Luke's appearance was much more chiselled. Luke looked like he had just walked off of a photoshoot with Vogue, whereas Sean had been boy-next-door handsome. They were opposites, and Laura couldn't help but wonder whether that was a good thing. Perhaps she needed something different to help her move on.

"I said we're here." He gestured out of the window to a modern-looking block of flats. A blush rose on Laura's cheeks. He was being kind and generous, allowing her to stay with him, meanwhile she was considering using him to move on from her possibly dead boyfriend. The morphine was confusing Laura's thoughts, and she no longer knew what she wanted.

"Oh, thank you." She climbed out of the taxi, with some help.

"Luke, I promise I'll pay you back for all this when I can access my accounts." Laura glanced down at her shoes as she stood to the side and watched Luke pay the taxi driver before he helped her into the building and led her to the lift. She had a sick feeling in her stomach that she was taking advantage of his kindness.

"Please, Claire, don't worry about it." Before Laura could respond, the lift doors pinged open onto the fifth floor and Luke stepped out, putting his hand in front of the doors so that Laura could safely hobble out on her crutches. She would have to tell him the truth about her name soon. After everything he was doing for her, he deserved to know the real her.

Laura followed Luke over to flat number forty. Even the front door looked expensive. As she followed him into the flat, she couldn't help but compare it with her old home. Instead of the plush beige carpets that her and Sean had chosen, Luke's flat had expensive looking wood flooring running throughout, effortlessly merging into each room. It was open plan, with both the living room, dining room and kitchen all in one. An estate agent would most likely refer to it as the perfect area to entertain in. Laura wondered whether Luke did much entertaining.

"The guest bedroom is just through here." Laura was eager to explore the whole flat, however she dutifully followed Luke into the bedroom. It was just like being in a posh hotel. The floor was the same dark wood as the rest of the flat, meanwhile the walls were various shades of white. She suspected they would describe the guest bedroom as 'brilliant white', otherwise known as 'bland'. The furniture looked expensive, and yet the room had no personality to it. It was similar to staying in a chain hotel, where guests expected the same room to be replicated wherever they were in the world.

"There's an ensuite just through that door, and the door to the left is the wardrobe. I'll let you get settled and order some dinner, are you happy with Indian?" Laura nodded in agreement, feeling a little overwhelmed at the life she had walked into. Who knew that getting hit by a bus could bring such luxury into your life? Not to mention a good looking and charming doctor.

Laura unpacked her few possessions and changed into an old pair of shorts that were at the bottom of her backpack. It was hot in the flat and other than the tattered jogging bottoms she had worn home from the hospital; she had nothing else that would go over her cast. Laura briefly glanced in the mirror, but her reflection repulsed her. She didn't recognise the gaunt face staring back at her with strands of lank blonde hair stuck to her face. Turning back into the bedroom, Laura looked towards the French doors which led out onto a balcony. There was something unnerving about it, she was exposed. Laura had to take a deep breath and remind herself that there was no way those men could know where she was. Nobody had followed them. Perhaps she wouldn't tell Luke her real name, the less he knew about her the better. To him, she would always be Claire. That also meant that she couldn't get too close to him - there was no chance of them having a future together.

CHAPTER SEVEN

The next few days were strange. Laura was reluctant to leave the flat in case anyone recognised her. Whilst she was in this concrete tower she was safe, nobody could find her. She'd left no clues at the hospital and so for now she could relax and enjoy feeling somewhat safe. Luke had been into work every day, leaving Laura to enjoy the quietness of his flat. She had almost forgotten what silence was. Having lived on the streets of London and in hostels for a year, she had grown accustomed to there always being noise coming from someone or somewhere.

Laura's first night in the flat had been peaceful. She thought she might struggle to sleep through fear of someone finding her, however as soon as her head hit the pillow she was asleep. There was something about Luke's company that made her feel safe. The following day had been difficult, left alone, with no distractions. She had only her own thoughts to keep her company, and that scared Laura. She hadn't wanted to be a burden to Luke and so she had spent the day curled up on the sofa flicking through the television channels. The old her would have hated spending a day like this, however there was nothing else she could do.

On that first day, before Luke came home, Laura took in her surroundings properly. She tiptoed around the flat, which was difficult considering her leg was in plaster, still afraid that someone might find her. The walls of his flat were surprisingly bare, not one picture hung on them. Laura reasoned with herself that perhaps it was because he was a single man who went out to work each day. He probably came home so tired every night that he didn't even realise that his walls were a blank canvas. No pictures stood on surfaces, only a few little nicknacks and a vase full of flowers. The flat was clean, tidy and somewhat clinical, but perhaps that was just a reflection of Luke. For now, it was a safe haven for Laura to recuperate in.

The first two days, Laura barely saw Luke. He had already left for work by the time she woke and both days he had left her a note saying he was having to work late. On her second day, waking up in Luke's flat, she woke up to find a note from him. He had left her one of his old mobiles. She picked it up. The phone was an old one of Luke's and could only send texts and make phone calls. It reminded Laura of a burner phone. She turned it over in her hands and considered how strange it was that something that had once been an integral part of her daily life now felt unusual in her grasp. The screen flashed, and Laura unlocked it to see that she already had one new message; it was from Luke.

Sorry I've not been around much. I thought I'd dig out this phone so at least we can text on my breaks. Let me know if you want anything from the shops on my way home. Luke xx

Laura couldn't help the butterflies in her stomach as she kept glancing at the kisses Luke had put at the end of the message. She tried to reason with herself that he was just being kind. It didn't work. Instead, Laura used her crutches to walk over to the sofa and sat down to text him back. She put three kisses at the end of her message. Laura spent most of the day staring at the phone, waiting for Luke to message her.

On Laura's third day at the flat, she woke to the sound of Luke preparing his breakfast in the kitchen and so she quickly dragged herself out of bed, wanting to briefly see him before he went out to work.

"Sorry, did I wake you?" asked Luke as she made her way into the kitchen, still trying to adjust to walking with the heavy cast on her leg.

"I was already awake." Laura lied, she didn't want him to feel awkward in his own home.

"I'm only in for a few hours this morning, so I thought we could spend the afternoon together?" There was a nervous edge to Luke's tone as he looked down at his bowl of cereal.

"That sounds perfect. Movies and a takeaway?" It was what Laura had been doing for the last two days, but to have Luke with her would make it so much more enjoyable.

"You can choose the film." Luke gave her a quick smile before going to grab his coat and leaving for the morning. Laura couldn't help the bubble of excitement that was rising within her. An entire afternoon in Luke's company!

Usually, after breakfast, Laura would collapse in front of the television and watch the first trashy program that she stumbled upon. Today, however, was different. She had an afternoon with Luke to get ready for. She decided to brave a shower. Laura knew she would have to keep her cast dry, and so she went to the cupboard under the sink, hoping that was where Luke kept his bin bags. To her delight she swung open the cupboard and right in front of her was a roll of bin bags. However, what struck Laura as odd was that there was nothing else in there. Didn't everyone keep their cleaning products in the cupboard under the sink? She shrugged to herself. Perhaps he had a cleaner who brought their own products with them. Once showered, Laura collapsed onto the bed, she was exhausted from her morning of activities, usually by now she'd be on her third episode of *Escape to the Country*.

Laura didn't have a hairbrush with her, and so she had a quick look through the drawers in her room. Maybe there was a hairdryer in there. She was wrong. Each drawer was completely empty. Luke really was a fan of minimalist living. Accepting her hair's frizzy, unbrushed fate, Laura made herself a coffee and sat down on the sofa, ready to find their first film of the evening. Thankfully, Luke had *Netflix* since he didn't own a single DVD. A sense of guilt washed over Laura for wasting these days and not looking for more information on Sean. However, she was enjoying having a break from the constant heartache.

CHAPTER EIGHT

Laura had only just sat down when Luke came bursting through the door, full of smiles and relief at his shift being over for the day. Laura was in awe of how hard he had been working all week.

"I bought movie snacks!" he announced, placing a bag filled with food on the sofa next to her.

"Could you get anymore perfect?" Laura kept her tone light, but she meant every word. Luke had picked up popcorn, an assortment of chocolate, various bottles of drinks, and the cherry on the top were the ingredients that he had picked up to make nachos.

"Are you ready for our movie marathon?" Luke asked, as he walked back into the room, now wearing jogging bottoms and an old faded t-shirt.

"I am! I thought we'd start off with something funny and so I've opted for *The Inbetweeners Movie*." Choosing a film had been difficult. Usually, Laura would opt for a Rom-Com, but something about curling up on the sofa with Luke and watching a cheesy romance seemed wrong. Perhaps because she had done it so many times with Sean that to do it with another man would be wrong.

"Perfect choice!"

They both settled into the film, relaxed in each other's company, as they laughed in-between devouring the mountain of food that Luke had brought home with him.

"Tell me about yourself." The film had ended, and Laura was staring at Luke's profile as he scrolled through Netflix, trying to find their next film.

"What do you want to know?" he asked her, shooting her one of his killer smiles. A blush crossed Laura's cheeks as his gaze settled on her. She couldn't tear her eyes from his.

The movie boomed in the background, making Laura jump. "Why don't you tell me about your family and your childhood?" Laura asked, trying to dispel the attraction between them.

"Okay, but it's not very exciting. As you've probably guessed, I had a very middle-class upbringing. I was as-good-as an only child, my older brother moved out before I was even old enough to remember. My dad is business minded, I suppose you could call him an entrepreneur. He was quite different to my mum. Mum was a doctor and wanted to help everyone, whereas dad is ruthless. I want to make them both proud, but it's difficult. During her spare time, my mother helped at the local homeless shelter and I would sometimes go along with her. She inspired me to want to help people and improve their lives." Luke's face remained humble throughout as his eyes shone with unshed tears. Laura had noticed that he spoke about his mother in the past tense.

"I'm sorry, Luke." She reached across and took his hand in hers, wanting to convey her emotions in the small gesture. His hand was soft and her hand fit perfectly in his.

"It's okay. She was a wonderful woman and she's the reason I'm a doctor. Anyway, enough about me. What about you, Claire? What skeletons do you have hidden in your closet?" Luke was smiling and his tone was light, but Laura couldn't help but freeze at his choice of words. Did he know she was keeping secrets from him?

Laura panicked, if she was going to tell him the truth about who she was then now would be the time to do it. Did she want to? Yes, he was gorgeous and had gone out of his way to help her, but could she trust him? She didn't know if she could trust anyone. In that split second she knew she couldn't tell anyone the truth, at least not until she was truly safe.

"There's not much to it. I was an only child. My parents brought me up in the centre of Manchester and I had a pet dog to keep me company." Laura saw the rejection flash across Luke's face. He knew she was holding back information. He was right, everything she had told him was a lie. She wasn't an only child. At the age of ten, her life had been turned on its head when her parents arrived home from the hospital with her baby brother in tow. She also had not lived in the centre of Manchester, and she had grown up with a cat, not a dog. Laura had lied, and she had also opted to keep up the facade of being called Claire. She didn't know whether the lies were to protect herself or to protect Luke, after all, the less he knew the better for him.

They spent the rest of the afternoon and evening watching films and eating nachos. Despite their earlier attempts at getting to know each other better, the conversation remained light and Luke told Laura about some of the most awkward patients he had looked after.

"Have you taken many of us awkward patients home?" Laura joked, but she saw a look of seriousness cross Luke's face.

"No, you're my first. I couldn't just leave a pretty girl like you to fend for herself on the streets with a broken ankle and a group of thugs after her." His eyes locked with hers and Laura's body fizzed with anticipation. His hand reached out to hold hers and a smile spread across her face at his touch. This time, she couldn't tear her eyes away from his. She felt compelled towards him. Slowly, she leaned into him and he met her halfway. It was nothing like kissing Sean. There was no familiarity about Luke's lips as he kissed her and she kissed him back. Laura had to admit he was a good kisser, possibly better than Sean, but it was wrong. She would trade a million kisses with Luke for just one with Sean. Laura pulled back and blinked a few times as she tried to find the words to soften the rejection.

"Sorry, I shouldn't have done that." Luke apologised, he looked embarrassed at how he had behaved.

"No, it's not your fault, Luke. I wanted to kiss you, but I just don't think I'm ready. I've been through a lot." Laura didn't want to talk to Luke about Sean and so she stood up, picked up her crutches and left him sitting alone, staring at a blank screen.

Once in bed, with the television switched on for background noise, Laura allowed the pain to knock down her walls. What had she been thinking kissing Luke? She wasn't even sure she trusted him. It upset her to think that Sean was no longer the last person she had kissed. She had betrayed him, and for what? A stupid fling that could never go anywhere. She would apologise tomorrow and tell him it couldn't happen again. Kissing Luke had taught her that Sean was her true soulmate and without him a piece of her was missing. Laura longed to pick up her phone and call Sean. They had been together for so long that she always went to him with her problems. Although, this was one problem he couldn't help her with. Her heart was being torn in two. One side wanted to find Sean, whilst the other wanted to seize life and live again.

CHAPTER NINE

The following morning was awkward. It was Luke's day off, however he had received a call asking him to go in. Laura wondered whether he had offered his help after their encounter last night.

"I should be home early tonight so I thought perhaps we could get a takeaway and try to forget about how awkward last night ended?" His voice was soft, but his brow knitted together and his eyes held a shimmer of regret. Laura had to shake her head to stop herself from falling under his spell.

"That sounds good, but why don't I cook for you instead?" She may as well make some use of her years of training to become a chef.

"Perfect. I'll see you around five." With a last smile and a wave of his hand, Laura watched as Luke left the flat. She couldn't help but feel a little upset at his absence. It had been so long since she had someone to speak to. However, perhaps a day apart would be good for them. It might help to dispel the atmosphere.

Feeling brave, Laura got dressed for the day and to pop out to a supermarket to buy the ingredients for dinner. She would have to go back out into the world at some point. She couldn't keep putting it off, and she wouldn't be able to stay indefinitely with Luke. With this in mind, Laura threw on her tatty jogging bottoms and grabbed the emergency cash Luke had left her. One day she hoped she would be able to access her own money to pay him back, but until then she would have to be in his debt.

As the fresh air hit Laura, her hands shook, and her breathing quickened. She was exposed now and did not know who knew of her whereabouts. She wondered whether anyone at the hospital had alerted the police to what had happened. If they had, then the police would be looking for her. Laura knew she would have to be careful. She had thrown on one of Luke's hoodies before leaving. She pulled the hood over her head, trying to cover her features. Laura didn't know the area and so she followed the crowd, hoping it would lead her to some shops. She was jumpy and couldn't help but feel as though someone was following her, however she tried to reassure herself that it was completely normal to feel that way after all she had been through.

Relief flooded her as she soon came across a small Tesco store. It would have everything she needed to make dinner. Quickly, she filled her basket. There were a few people that she kept seeing, but she wasn't sure whether they were following her or if they were just doing their weekly shop. She was feeling incredibly paranoid and so Laura made her way to the check-out and paid for her ingredients, putting them into a backpack to carry home. On her way back to the flat she walked towards the oncoming crowd - a difficult feat when using crutches - hoping that it would offer her some protection. As she found herself back at the entrance to the flat, she looked behind her and fear flooded her body. Stood on the opposite side of the road, staring directly at her, was a man. Laura gasped for breath as she noticed the man was wearing the same uniform that the men at the hospital had been. He could have even been one of the men from the hospital.

Laura made her way into the flat, as quickly as possible, and locked the door firmly behind her. However, it wasn't until she got inside the flat she realised there could be someone inside waiting for her. Her heart hammered in her chest as she strained her ears to hear whether she was alone. She froze as she heard footsteps coming from the living room. A sick feeling settled in the pit of her stomach. Laura was trapped, the balcony was too high for her to jump, and the cast on her leg meant that she couldn't run anywhere. This was it. She was finally about to see Sean again. Perhaps the men would even tell her why they had killed Sean. At least then she would know what this was all about, even if it was too late.

With a sense of resignation, Laura put the bag of shopping down by the door and made her way to the living room. Inside she was falling apart, but she would not show them. She would pretend she was feeling brave. They had already taken Sean from her; she would not give them the satisfaction of watching her suffer.

"Where have you been? Are you okay?" Laura almost lost her footing as she heard Luke's voice. It was him in the living room, not somebody lurking, waiting to murder her.

"Oh, Luke!" Laura gasped as her body slumped against the wall. She couldn't control herself any longer as relief took over.

"Claire, what's wrong?" Luke asked, he pulled her into his embrace.

"They're outside." she whispered, trying to stop herself from sobbing into his chest.

"Let's sit you down." With a practiced efficiency, Luke calmly walked Laura over to the sofa and sat her down. He then went to make her a cup of tea, putting sugar in it to help with the shock. "Here, drink this. I'm going to call the police." He handed her the tea and picked up his phone, leaving the room as he dialled the number. Laura tried to focus on her breathing. She took long, deep breaths to slow her heart rate and calm herself down. By the time Luke returned, Laura had gained some control over herself and could form enough words to have a conversation.

"What did they say?" she asked, thoughts whirling around her head. Thankfully, Luke only knew her as Claire and so he couldn't give away her identity.

"I told them someone had followed me home from work. They're going to send an officer out straight away. In the meantime, we have to stay put."

"What about after? I can't stay here." As Laura said the words the reality set in, she was no longer safe here with Luke.

"I've thought about that. A friend of mine is on holiday at the moment and I have the keys to his flat, we can stay there."

Within a few minutes, they had both packed a bag and were sitting back in the living room trying to devise a plan as to how they would leave without anyone seeing them.

"You're overthinking things, Claire. I have a car parked in the basement garage, we'll be able to take the lift straight down there and drive away. Nobody will expect you to leave the building in a car." Laura had to admit that Luke made a valid argument.

"How will we know when it's safe?" Laura asked, her voice trembling with fear. She had always suspected that this day would come, where they caught up with her, but the reality was so much worse than what she had been expecting.

Luke didn't answer her question, instead he took her hand in his and squeezed. The awkward atmosphere had disappeared, and he was back to being kind and attentive.

CHAPTER TEN

After what seemed like an eternity, but was probably only an hour or two, Laura and Luke made their way down to the carpark in the building's basement. Laura wondered whether she should feel scared. A complete stranger was about to put her in a car and drive her to an unknown destination. However, Laura couldn't feel scared. Luke had been lovely to her, incredibly helpful, and he had even saved her life. She knew he was on her side. The men who were after her were much scarier, and for now, that was reason enough for Laura to trust Luke.

Luke led Laura to a fancy Range Rover, which looked as though he rarely used it. There wasn't a single fingerprint on the shiny black exterior. With a flick of a button, the boot opened and Luke stashed their bags. He then walked around to the passenger side to help Laura climb into the car - it wasn't an easy feat with a heavy cast on her leg. He then took her crutches from her and laid them down on the backseat. She would miss having someone to look after her when she inevitably had to leave Luke.

"Are you okay?" Luke asked once they were both seated in the car and had their seat belts on.

"I think so," whispered Laura as she watched Luke man-oeuvre the car out of the parking space and towards the exit. She was grateful that the car had tinted windows so that even if anyone spotted them, it was unlikely they would be able to see who the occupants were. Laura had one of Luke's baseball caps on, and she had sunk down in the seat so that nobody could see her face.

"It's going to be okay." Luke reassured her as they drove out into daylight and quickly merged with the London traffic. There didn't seem to be anybody around watching them.

"Tell me more about yourself to distract me, please." Finding out more about Luke was a pleasant distraction.

"Fun fact, I'm a black belt in karate." That hadn't been what Laura had been expecting Luke to say, but it immediately provided some reassurance. Those men that had been in the hospital didn't look as though they could run to the toilet, let alone fight against black-belt Luke.

They both lapsed into silence as Luke navigated his way through the bustling roads of London, whilst Laura conjured up images of a topless Luke doing karate. She knew, strictly speaking, he wouldn't be topless, but in a situation like this, where her life was in danger, she was sure the karate gods would be okay with it.

"I also make an amazing roast dinner," Luke announced, shattering Laura's carefully thought-through karate fantasy.

"I love a roast dinner," Laura commented as her stomach rumbled. Her mind wandered to Sunday lunches at Luke's father's house with his family around. She wondered whether it would feel as homely as Sunday lunch at Sean's had been. They had been together for so long that his parents treated her as one of their own children. She never left their house without a big smile on her face and a huge bowl of leftovers for Monday night's dinner. Laura bit her lip until she drew blood. She had to stop her mind wandering to Sean. Her fantasies about Luke were pointless, even if things were different and he knew the real her. It was too late. Laura's heart was broken, and it already belonged to someone else.

The journey didn't take long, every time the car slowed to a stop Laura would glance around them to see if she recognised any cars following them. Thankfully, it didn't look like anyone was.

"I'm afraid there's no parking at the flat so we'll just have to find a spot along the street." Luke's apologetic tone reverberated through Laura, he was being incredibly thoughtful towards her feelings. He knew how scared she was. All this was for her, and yet she was putting him in immense danger. She didn't know how she could ever thank him for his help.

Luke effortlessly parked the car along a quaint road filled with smart-looking townhouses. It was early afternoon and people were at work, so the street was quiet. They both sat for a moment, taking in their surroundings and breathing a sigh of relief that nobody had ambushed them on the journey. As they sat in silence, a memory tried to break into Laura's consciousness. It was the night she came home from hospital. The night Luke told her he didn't own a car.

"Luke, I thought you said you didn't have a car?" Laura's voice trembled. He had lied to her, and she wasn't sure she wanted to know the reason behind it.

"I meant I didn't have a car at the hospital." He smiled over at her, but it seemed false. An involuntary shiver ran through Laura's body. She decided not to mention the car again.

Without saying another word, they both climbed out of the car and Luke took their bags from the boot. He pointed to a house a few doors down and Laura followed him. Her eyes were darting around them to see whether there was anyone around who could have followed them. She followed Luke up the path and he unlocked the front door, which opened onto a small hallway.

"It's flat one, the door is straight ahead." He took out a set of keys and let her into the flat. Laura was relieved to see that it was on the ground floor. That made running away easier - at least it would if she didn't have a broken ankle.

Following Luke into the flat, Laura couldn't help but notice the similarities to Luke's own home. The walls were bare and there were very few personal pictures or possessions. It was almost like walking into a show home. Perhaps his friend was another busy doctor. Laura cast her thoughts aside as she sat down in the living room and Luke came to sit beside her.

"What now?" she asked, she wasn't expecting an answer, she was merely thinking aloud.

"Claire, I think you better tell me a little more about what's going on." Laura knew there would come a time when Luke asked more questions, and after all he had done for her, she knew she had to tell him. She had known him for almost a week now, and all he had done was worry about her and ensure she was safe. It was time to share her story with him.

"Okay, I'm not sure where to begin." Laura took a deep breath as she tried to organise her thoughts. She would tell Luke everything except her identity. If he had to get the police involved, then at least he wouldn't be able to tell them who she was.

"Start at the beginning, it's okay, Claire, I'm here." He reached out and took her hands in his. It was intended to be a comforting gesture, however it just made her heart beat faster and further confused her thoughts.

"27th October 2019. That was the day it happened, the day my life fell apart." Laura took a deep breath. Was she really about to tell an almost-stranger about the most traumatic day of her life? She had to. He was her only help right now and he couldn't continue to help her without knowing what, or who, they were running from. Laura took a deep breath and told Luke about the night she came home to find a pool of blood and no Sean.

"I'm sorry for your loss." Luke's face was ashen, as though he was experiencing her pain with her. There was something cathartic about telling someone what she had gone through.

"That's the thing, we don't know if we lost him. They never found a body." Laura had to dampen down the hope that always swelled inside of her whenever this little detail came up. Just because they hadn't found Sean's body didn't mean that he was alive. The people had broken into the flat knew what they were doing, as did the ones who were following her. It was likely that they knew exactly how to cover their tracks. Then there was the further evidence that the police had which led to Sean being presumed dead. Laura wasn't sure she wanted to know what that further evidence was.

"Why did they target him?" asked Luke. He was careful how he worded his question.

"That's my biggest question. To this day, I don't know why this happened to him. How stupid is it I'm on the run from a group of criminals but I don't even know why?" Laura's body sunk into the chair as she was overcome by exhaustion, she had been so brave until that moment, but now the crushing feeling of loss overcame her. Luke pulled her into his warm embrace. It was nice to have someone hold and comfort her. "I've searched for over a year now, but I can't find any answers. I'm desperate to know what happened and why, but I don't know where to turn next."

After a few minutes, she pulled back from his embrace. She needed to control her emotions. Talking about Sean hurt. Taking a deep breath, she shut the feelings of loss away in a little compartment in her brain. Those feelings would only stop her from thinking clearly, and right now she needed to come up with a plan on how she was going to escape this mess. As she stared at Luke's face, only a few inches from her own, his arms were still wrapped around her. Guilt crushed Laura's heart. How could she have dragged such a kind and thoughtful man into this mess? His green eyes gazed into hers and she couldn't look away. His fingers traced their way up her arm leaving her skin fizzing from his touch. She didn't know who moved first, although she was sure it couldn't have been her, but his lips were on hers and he was kissing her. It took Laura a moment to respond - she kissed him back.

Her mind was confused and the pain of Sean's loss was ripping her apart, but for those few short moments, Luke silenced everything. She found a brief escape.

The kiss only lasted a few seconds before Laura's senses returned, and she pulled back. Luke was a lovely and thoughtful man, but she couldn't do this. She couldn't betray Sean. Despite over a year apart, she still loved him and she would still give anything to have him back in her life. The kiss with Luke had been lovely, but it wasn't right. Their last kiss had already complicated their relationship, they didn't need anymore problems right now.

"I'm so sorry." Luke gasped as he moved back on the sofa to put some distance between the two of them.

"It's okay." Laura replied, her voice was small and full of emotion. She didn't know what to say. It was not Luke's fault, but it was the wrong thing to do.

"No, it's not okay. You were vulnerable, and I took advantage." The pain on Luke's face shocked Laura. She didn't want him to feel guilty for something that wasn't his fault. If the situation was different, then Laura knew she could be very happy with Luke. It was complicated and messy. Life didn't get much more complicated than being on the run.

"Honestly, Luke, it's fine. I'm going to go for a lie down, today's taken it out of me. Why don't you order us some dinner and come and get me once it's here?" Laura needed a few minutes alone. She wanted to shut herself away and cry. It wasn't often she allowed the full force of her feelings to invade her thoughts, but when she did, the feeling of loss was suffocating. The reminder she had to go on living without Sean by her side was by far the worst feeling she had ever encountered.

Laura laid down on the single bed in the middle of the guest bedroom. Luke had tried to give her the main bedroom, but she had refused. The stress of the day caught up with her and she laid there and sobbed until her throat was raw and there were no tears left to fall. She pressed her fingers to her lips. Why had she allowed Luke to kiss her? The first time had been a mistake, the second time should never have happened. As she sat there alone, listening to the surrounding city, she thought back to the first time Sean had kissed her, twelve years ago.

1st June 2008,

"Are you asking me on a date?" Seventeen-year-old Laura twirled a strand of hair around her finger. Her friend Rachel had told her it made girls look sophisticated and sexy. Laura suspected she just looked silly as she tried to untangle the hair from her finger. Sean Scott was standing in front of her, dangling his car keys at her. It was their last ever day of school and they had both just walked out of their final A-level exam. As Laura was walking down the hallway, Sean had caught up with her and asked her if she wanted to grab a coffee.

"Do you want me to ask you on a date?" he had teased her, falling into stride beside her.

"Ask me and you'll find out." Laura had finally pulled her finger free of her hair. She wouldn't be trying that again.

"Laura Harper, will you go on a date with me to get a cup of coffee?" To Laura's horror, Sean had taken her hand and got

down on one knee, embarrassing her in front of everyone. At least it would have been embarrassing if Laura cared what anyone else thought. Instead, she burst out laughing and told Sean that she would love to go on a date with him.

As Sean drove them into town, Laura didn't stop laughing. They had always been friends, however over the last few months they had grown closer. Once in town, they headed to Laura's favourite cafe where she knew for a fact that they did the best hot chocolate in the north.

"What would you like?" Sean asked as they chose a table by the window.

"Could I have a hot chocolate with cream and marshmallows?" She beamed back at him. Nobody could be unhappy around Sean, his enthusiasm for life was contagious.

"Hot chocolate, in June?" Sean didn't look convinced, but he shrugged his shoulders and went over to order at the counter. Whilst she waited for him to return, Laura couldn't help but stare at Sean. He was eighteen, with short brown hair, an athletic build, vivid blue eyes and a wicked sense of humour. He towered above her short frame, and Laura could only imagine how lovely it would feel to have him embrace her. They had been friends for long enough for her to know that he was a good person, with an amazing personality, and he never failed to make her laugh.

"Hot chocolate, in June," Sean announced as he placed two identical mugs down on the table. Laura raised her eyebrows at him. "I couldn't let you drink alone." He shrugged his shoulders and sat down opposite her.

They sat at that table until the cafe closed, and not once did the smile fall from Laura's face. Sean had agreed that hot chocolate in summer was acceptable after taking the first sip of the delectable drink. They discussed their futures and realised that whilst most of their friends were heading off to university, they were both staying home to pursue their careers. Laura was to attend the local college to study catering - she hoped to get an internship at a restaurant. Meanwhile, Sean was joining the police force.

Sean drove her home and Laura revelled in every second they spent in each other's company. She didn't want the evening to end.

"Laura, do you have plans for tomorrow?" Sean's face looked apprehensive as he waited for her reply. It was Friday night and with the entire summer stretching ahead of her before she started college, Laura had very few plans, other than cooking and trying lots of new foods.

"That depends." She smiled back at him. She would not let him get away with it that easily.

"Depends on what?" he asked, looking a little deflated.

"On whether you're going to ask me out on another date." She saw the flash of happiness across his face as he realised what she was saying.

"Laura Harper, would you do me the honour of going on another date with me tomorrow?" Thankfully, they were still sitting in Sean's car and so he could not bend down on one knee again.

"I'd love to." She smiled back at him. Excitement was already building inside of her. Another day with Sean Scott, this was definitely going to be a summer to remember.

"I'll pick you up at midday. I've been wanting to try out a new restaurant and I suspect you're just the girl to take with me." Before Laura could reply, Sean had leaned over and planted his lips on hers. Being the awkward teenager that she was, Laura froze, waiting for her brain to kick in.

"Are you going to kiss me back?" Sean asked, pulling back from her slightly.

"Sorry, you just took me by surprise." Laura blushed.

"No, that's okay. I shouldn't have been so presumptuous as to kiss you." It was Sean's turn to look embarrassed now.

"No, Sean, I want to kiss you." Laura was horrified at the giggle that escaped her lips as she leaned over to kiss Sean.

It may not have been the perfect first kiss, but it was perfect for them. It had completely summed up their relationship, playful and caring.

CHAPTER ELEVEN

"Claire, dinner's here!" Luke called from outside her bedroom door.

"Thank you, I'll be right out." Laura rubbed her puffy eyes and swung her legs off of the bed. She would be brave and face Luke. She deeply regretted kissing him for a second time. There was no denying that he was attractive. Laura was confused and hurt, all she wanted was for Sean to wrap his arms around her and tell her that everything would be okay. She craved the feeling of someone caring for her. Laura couldn't imagine what it would feel like to never feel Sean's arms around her again. The thought alone brought a lump to her throat. To never gaze into his eyes again or to feel his touch - it was unbearable. She had to be brave and keep searching for answers.

Laura walked into the living room to find Luke sat down with two pizza boxes and two bottles of beer. He was flicking through the television channels as she sat down next to him.

"I've got a Margherita and a four cheese, which one would you like?" Always the gentleman - unless he was trying to kiss you - Luke held out the boxes, waiting for Laura to make her choice.

"The Margherita, please." Laura had never been very adventurous in her pizza choices, something that Sean marvelled at, given her career as a chef.

Laura took a bite of the pizza and sighed in delight. After going so long not knowing when her next meal would be, she knew how lucky she was to have so much food in front of her. They ate in silence for a while, neither of them knowing what to say. Laura had never been in a situation like this, and so she did not know what the best way to deal with it was.

"I'm sorry." Luke's voice was almost a whisper as he paused in-between pizza slices. Laura finished the mouthful she was chewing, wondering what to say.

"Can we just forget about it? I could brush it off and say it's okay, but honestly, it's not. I shouldn't have done it, and I regret it. It's not your fault. Oh god, this is awful - I've turned this into an 'it's not you, it's me moment'." Laura sighed, she had just gone and made everything even more awkward.

Luke laughed. "Claire, calm down. I understand, you've been through a lot. Let's just forget it ever happened." He reached his hand out and Laura shook it in agreement.

"Would you like a beer?" Luke asked, pointing towards the second beer on the coffee table.

"I thought I couldn't drink with my pain meds?" When Luke had discharged her from the hospital, he had taken her to the pharmacy where they dispensed her medication. The pharmacist was very explicit in telling her that under no circumstances was she allowed to consume alcohol with them.

"I won't tell anyone if you don't." Luke winked at her. The pharmacist had repeated the warning twice. Despite Luke being a doctor, Laura didn't want to take any risks and so she declined.

"I'll be asleep in five seconds if I drink that," she joked, trying to dissipate the tension in the room. Why had he been trying to encourage her to drink?

Laura finished her pizza in silence as Luke diverted his attention towards the television. She was feeling increasingly uneasy in his presence, but wasn't sure why. There had been a few strange occurrences, but nothing out of the ordinary. She had to keep reminding herself that he had saved her life, so why would he want to harm her?

CHAPTER TWELVE

The following morning, Laura walked into the kitchen to find Luke sat at the table eating his breakfast. In silence, she poured herself a cup of coffee and sat down at the table. Despite them sharing a takeaway last night, there was still an awkward atmosphere lingering. Laura was feeling uneasy around Luke. There was also something off about him. Last night had only emphasised that. However, until she knew the truth behind Sean's disappearance, and possible death, she had no other choice but to trust him. Last night's reminiscing had reminded her just how much she missed Sean and wanted him back in her life. They had shared many happy memories together, and she still couldn't see her future without him in it.

"I'm sorry about yesterday." Luke said, looking up from his bowl of cereal. He had dark circles under his eyes and kept running his fingers through his hair.

"Please, Luke, let's not dwell on it. We made a mistake, but we can move on from that mistake. Friends?" Luke nodded in agreement.

"We really need to come up with a plan, Claire. What do you want to achieve? Do you want to find out what happened to your boyfriend, or do you want to just live in peace?" Luke's question set Laura's mind racing. What did she want? She had never really considered it that way, she had always assumed that she would have to discover the truth before she could live in peace. Laura knew that discovering what happened was the only option. She had to know what happened to Sean, and then she could start thinking about the future.

"I want both, but I'm not sure whether that's possible."

"Anything's possible, we just need to come up with a plan." He smiled at her and immediately Laura blushed. She was doing that a lot around Luke.

"Luke, please don't take this the wrong way because I really appreciate your help. I'm just wondering why you're helping me? I've put you in serious danger. You should run as far away as possible." Laura wrapped her hands around her warm cup of coffee for comfort. A stranger was her best hope of getting out of this mess alive, and not only did that scare her, but it also made her feel awfully lonely. She had to know the reasons behind his actions before she could truly trust him.

"I'm a doctor, it's in my nature to help people. My mother also brought me up to be kind and considerate towards others. I know she would be proud of me if she were here to see me helping you. Besides, they were watching my flat so I can't exactly go back. From a selfish point of view, I've got to help you to help me." Despite the gravity of his words, Luke kept his expression light and cheerful. A crushing guilt still engulfed Laura as she thought of how she had dragged Luke into this awful mess. He was too caring for his own good, and it had got him into trouble.

"So, what do we do next?" It was nice to know that she

would have someone by her side again. There was a certain safety in numbers, especially when number two was a tall doctor with a black belt in karate.

"What happened to the flat you shared with Sean?"

Laura thought for a few moments, she didn't know what had happened. Had her parents and Sean's parents cleared it? Could they have sold it without her there and no confirmation of Sean's death? Or perhaps it was still part of the criminal investigation?

"I'm not sure," she admitted. She couldn't bear the thought of someone else living in her flat. Despite the horrific memories of that night, the flat held so many incredible happy memories.

"I have some contacts. Why don't you write the address down on this piece of paper and I'll see what I can discover."

Laura wondered what connections Luke had that could find out who, if anyone, was living at a particular address. However, she reasoned with herself that being a doctor, he probably had contacts in the police. As Luke went outside to make his call, Laura stayed sat at the kitchen table staring down at her cup of coffee. Something about that morning jogged her memory, and she was immediately taken back to a morning a few days before Sean's disappearance.

24th October 2019,

It was a rare morning where Sean was not on an early shift or tucked up in bed having worked through the night. For once, they could sit and eat breakfast together. At least, that was what Laura had been planning on doing, until Sean's phone rang and he crept out of the flat. Laura had sat there and picked at her croissant, wondering who he could be on the phone to that meant he had to leave the flat. Over the years, Sean had taken many confidential work phone calls with her in earshot. She couldn't help the fear that bubbled away inside of her, gnawing at her insides. If it wasn't work, then what was it? Was he having an affair? The thought flitted across Laura's mind, but she quickly pushed it to the side. Of course Sean wasn't having an affair, he loved her. Didn't he? He wouldn't just throw away an eleven-year-old relationship.

By the time Sean returned to the flat, the fresh croissants were cold, the coffee had stagnated and Laura was pulling on her coat, ready to leave for a day at work. It would be late by the time she returned and Sean would most likely be asleep as he had an early start the following day. For the first time in their relationship, Laura was awkward around him, unsure of how to act or what questions to ask him.

"You okay?" he asked, stepping towards her. Laura couldn't help but flinch back. It was a natural reaction, but one that she had never experienced in the presence of Sean.

"Are you okay?" she returned his question, taking in his appearance. There was something about him that looked hassled. He had beads of sweat forming on his head despite the chilly October temperatures. His eyes were darting towards the door like he wanted to leave.

"I'm fine. What's going on, Laura?" Despite the look of worry in his eyes, his tone was harsh and not how he would usually speak to her.

"What's going on? What's going on with you, Sean?" she retorted. It hurt for him to speak to her like this, as if she were annoying him with trivial questions. It wasn't the Sean she knew.

"Sorry, Laura, it's just work." He sighed and his whole demeanour changed. His body relaxed, his eyes softened and the creases in his forehead flattened. He stepped forward, and this time Laura let him wrap his arms around her. The familiar feeling of his embrace, and the smell of his aftershave calmed her. This was her Sean, he would never hurt her. These late nights were playing havoc with her mind.

"Do you want to talk about it?" She didn't really have time to sit and talk, but she knew she had to try. There was obviously something worrying him.

"No, it's fine. I'll be okay in a few days, just a stressful operation that they have assigned me to." He gave her a reassuring smile and pulled her in for another hug - Laura didn't know whether the hug was for her benefit or his.

"I'm here if you need to chat, okay?"

"I know, now get to work before you're late!" He walked her towards the door and handed her bags to her.

"I love you." She smiled at him before reaching up on her tiptoes to give him a kiss goodbye.

"I love you too. Let's book that holiday when you get home tonight, I think we could do with a break." As Laura closed the door and walked towards her car, she couldn't wipe the smile off of her face. A holiday, somewhere hot, with Sean was just what she needed.

◆ ◆ ◆

The noise of a car horn jolted Laura back to the present. She gasped for breath. Laura hated how these flashbacks would take her over and then leave her feeling heartbroken. They never booked that holiday. When she got home that night there was a note from Sean apologising that he had to work late. There was nothing unusual about that note, but Laura's heart had sunk. In that moment, she knew something was going on. Somehow, those memories and those feelings had been lost under the grief and trauma. Now they were coming back to her, she was sure that something had been going on. What had Sean been involved in that had led to this happening? She almost wished it had been another woman.

"I've got good news!" Luke called as he walked back into the flat.

"Your contact had information?" Laura asked, she wanted to know more about this contact but she had too much whirling around inside of her head to add anything more to it.

"Yes. You and Sean still own the flat, and nobody else is living there."

The uneasiness resurfaced within Laura. How did a doctor know somebody who could access so much information with such ease?

CHAPTER THIRTEEN

All too soon, their bags were packed, and they were in the car hurtling towards Manchester. Luke had promised Laura that he had lots of holiday to take from work and they wouldn't miss him. Despite Luke's profession and the number of traffic accident victims he must have tended to, he was paying little notice to the speed limit. Laura couldn't help but observe how his hands gripped the steering wheel, his knuckles were almost white. The stress of the last few days had caught up with Laura. She was tired, her heart was constantly pounding in her chest and she felt sick. She'd also had a few flashbacks to her life with Sean and they had completely drained her, both physically and emotionally. Something told Laura that this trip was about to change everything.

"What's our plan?" Laura asked, trying to distract herself from the uneasiness that was gnawing away in the pit of her stomach.

"I've booked us a hotel online. I thought we'd go there first, perhaps grab some food, and we'll go to the flat tonight, when it's dark." Luke didn't take his eyes off the road, he just kept staring ahead whilst talking. By now, he was weaving in and out of traffic, and Laura could only describe his driving as erratic.

"That sounds good." Laura didn't know what else to say.

It seemed Luke had already formed a plan without consulting her. They would have to be careful entering the flat in case anyone was searching for her.

They remained in silence for the rest of the journey. It was awkward, and Laura was relieved when they pulled up outside an average-looking hotel in the middle of Manchester. If Laura had been in charge of booking the hotel, she would have booked something on the outskirts of the city, but perhaps hiding in plain sight was better. With a quick glance around the car park, Laura clumsily climbed out of the car. There was nobody around. She took her crutches and prepared herself for the physical pain as she tried to keep up with Luke. Although her ribs were slowly healing, they were still painful, and the constant pain was exhausting.

"Have you stayed here before?" she asked Luke, not that she was particularly interested in his answer, she just wanted to end the strange silence that had fallen.

"No, I've only been to Manchester a handful of times. Have you stayed here before?" Luke grabbed their bags from the boot and walked towards the hotel. Laura struggled to keep up with his long-strides.

"I've never stayed here. I've never even noticed the hotel, and I must have walked past it a thousand times." Luke wasn't listening to her answer, he was already at the reception desk checking them in. Laura wasn't sure what had happened, but his attitude towards her had definitely shifted. Perhaps the gravity of their situation had hit him and he was regretting his decision in helping her. She didn't blame him, she wasn't sure she could put herself in danger for a complete stranger. Perhaps she was entirely misguiding him and he was feeling rejected after their kiss. Laura wasn't sure what was influencing his decisions, and she couldn't waste her energy on worrying about it.

Once they were up in the room, Laura was relieved to discover that there were separate beds. She took the one by the window and sat down for a moment to catch her breath. Thankfully, she still had some pain medication with her and so she delved inside her backpack for it.

"What do you fancy for lunch?" Luke asked her. He had a smile on his face again and the odd atmosphere had evaporated.

"Do they do room service?" They had a lot to discuss and Laura couldn't face trying to walk around Manchester with this cast on her leg. She needed some time to recuperate before they went out tonight.

An hour later, they were sitting at the small table in their room, each with a toasted cheese and ham sandwich and a side of chips in front of them. It wasn't exactly Cordon bleu, but it was just what they needed.

"Do you have the key to the flat?" Luke asked her. His eyes settled on hers. A chill ran down Laura's spine. She wanted to believe it was because an attractive man was staring at her, but she still had a strange feeling in her stomach.

"Yeah, I do. What time were you thinking of leaving?"

"Just after midnight?"

"Yeah, sure. Hopefully, all the neighbours will be indoors by then, I don't want any of them recognising me."

As Laura said the words out loud she realised that the chance of anybody recognising her was very slim - she was far from the happy woman that had once lived there with the love of her life. At the most, they might mistake her for a distant relative of the Laura Harper that once lived there.

They finished their meal in silence before agreeing to have a nap so that they were wide awake for their trip that evening. Once in bed, Laura couldn't switch off. Her brain had thoughts whizzing around at a hundred miles per hour. Eventually, she fell into a fitful sleep that was peppered with memories of her and Sean.

20th August 2019,

The sun shone down on Laura's back, making her smile. She was sitting on the edge of a river bank, enjoying the peace while Sean unpacked the picnic basket next to her. It was a rare day where the sun was shining and they both had the day off. They had packed a picnic and travelled to their favourite spot just outside the city.

"I don't think we'll ever need to eat again!" Sean laughed as he kept pulling food out of the basket. The chef inside of Laura had gone a little overboard when she packed their lunch. They had quiche, sandwiches, salads, pasta salads, olives, cheeses and fresh macarons for dessert.

"There'll be nothing left by the time you're finished." Laura teased him. Sean loved her cooking, and he had an enormous appetite.

"I can't help it, you just make such delicious food." Sean's

reply was muffled as he took a bite out of one of the sandwiches. It was mustard and cured ham on fresh granary bread, his favourite.

They had laid in the sun for hours, slowly grazing on the feast. The stresses of their working days ebbed away, and once again they were their carefree selves, enjoying each other's company with endless jokes and teasing.

"Laura, promise me if anything ever happens to me you'll protect yourself. Don't go looking for me." Sean had suddenly become serious - ruining the playful atmosphere that they had been indulging in all afternoon.

"Sean, don't be silly." Laura had disregarded his comment and leant forward to squeeze his hand. Nothing would ever happen to Sean. They had a lifetime together, and she intended to make the most of it.

"No. Laura, please, I need you to be serious for a moment." There was a look of desperation on Sean's face as he put down his drink and grasped both of Laura's hands in his.

"Sean, what's going on?" she asked him. The sudden shift in his mood had worried her. It was no secret that Sean's job was dangerous, but that was the risk that every police officer took. His face was scaring her, he looked so worried and stressed.

"It's just work, Laura, but you know how I worry and how much I worry about you. I love you so much, you have to promise me that if anything ever happens, you'll prioritise your safety above anything else."

"I promise," whispered Laura. She moved next to him and laid her head on his chest as he wrapped his arms around her. She laid there listening to his heartbeat for what seemed like *forever.*

"If I'm ever not there, keep Mr Ted safe." Laura had laughed at this remark. Mr Ted was a teddy bear Sean had won for her at the local summer fete. He had been incredibly proud of his win and had made sure everyone knew he had won it for Laura.

◆ ◆ ◆

Laura woke with a jolt, the room was dark but she could just about make out Luke's silhouette, sitting at the table looking at something on his phone. It took a moment for Laura to organise her thoughts. That dream had brought back the memories of that sunny August day that she had completely forgotten about. With the advantage of hindsight, Laura now wondered whether Sean had been giving her a clue. Could the teddy bear help her understand what was happening?

"Claire, you're awake. It's almost midnight." Luke smiled over at her, waiting for her to get ready to leave. Laura wasn't sure why, but she didn't think she should tell Luke about the teddy bear, at least not until she knew whether it was a clue.

CHAPTER FOURTEEN

Laura cursed the cast on her leg as she tried to keep up with Luke as they walked up to the entrance to the block of flats. She was about to walk back into her old life and back to the scene of the most traumatic event that she had ever experienced. Laura's heart was pounding in her chest, but she had to ignore it. There was no time for her to have an emotional breakdown - it would have to wait until later. Tonight was about finding out what happened to Sean.

"Do you have the fob to get in?" Luke asked her, reaching his hand out for the keys. Laura kept her grip on them and walked past him to open the door herself. These keys were the only item she had connecting herself to this flat and to Sean. She would keep them firmly in her own hands.

"It's this way." For once, Laura took the lead. This was her territory, and she had to show Luke that. He had shown a harsher side to himself, and Laura was starting to want to distance herself from him.

"It's a lovely building." Luke commented as he followed her into the lift. Laura had never really used the lift before, she was usually one to take the stairs.

"It is. We would walk past the building on our way to the pub and we'd always comment on how much we wanted to live here. It was like a dream come true when one of the flats came up for sale. Sean had already put an offer on the flat before he even took me to view it." A ghost of a smile crossed Laura's face as she thought about how Sean had surprised her on her birthday. He had pretended to take her to the pub, however as they walked past the building he buzzed the bell, took her up to the flat and announced that they were buying it.

"He sounds like the perfect boyfriend." The lift opened and Luke walked out first, holding the doors open for Laura to exit.

"He was." she replied, making her way towards the front door. Her front door. She knew she would have to be quick to scoop up any post to ensure that Luke didn't catch sight of her real name. That would raise too many questions and ones she didn't want to answer.

With a deep breath, Laura put the key in the lock and opened the door to her old flat. A musty smell hit her senses as she opened the door and swiftly bent down to scoop up the post on the welcome mat. There were only a few envelopes, Laura suspected that either her or Sean's parents had been coming and going from the flat. Pushing thoughts of her parents to the back of her mind, Laura promptly hid the letters from sight and breathed a sigh of relief that her and Sean hadn't been the type of couple that bought personalised gifts.

"Where should we look first?" Laura asked. She wanted to station Luke in another room so she could grab a backpack and put the teddy bear safely in it, ready for her to inspect at a later date.

"I'm not sure, Laura, it's your flat." Despite his apparent reluctance to rifle through her drawers, Laura could see Luke's eyes roaming around the flat. He was eager to pry into her personal life to see whether he could unearth some clues. Something about his tone threw Laura, but she quickly composed herself, ready to give him a task.

"You start in the living room and I'll look in the bedroom." The decision to send Luke into the living room went beyond just trying to get him out of the way. Laura wasn't sure whether she could face walking into that room, knowing it was possibly where Sean had lost his life.

They went their separate ways and Laura slowly wandered into the bedroom. She had to keep a tight grip on her emotions as the memories came flooding back. All the times she had come home from work late and Sean had already been cuddled up under the duvet. Or the mornings when he was on the late shift and he would wake her up with breakfast in bed. Why did her memories have to paint Sean in such a positive light? Yes, he had been an amazing boyfriend, but he wasn't without fault. However, losing him had highlighted just how insignificant those faults were.

Before Luke came looking for her, Laura grabbed a backpack from the wardrobe, a black Nike one that had been Sean's. Mr Ted was sitting on her bedside table and she quickly stuffed him into the bottom of the bag, alongside a framed picture of them. The picture had been taken at Sean's cousins's wedding. They were both beaming at the camera after a day of happiness and even talk of their own wedding. Laura had left that wedding feeling on top of the world and excited for their future together.

"Have you found anything?" Luke called, pulling her back to the present.

"Not yet, have you?" She shoved some clothes into the backpack and started going through drawers.

"Nothing of any significance."

As Laura went through the drawers in the bedroom, she noticed things were missing. She couldn't be sure it hadn't been her or Sean's family, however she doubted they would have taken iPads and fitness trackers, and left pictures. Perhaps Sean had information stored on them that people wanted. The gang had already ransacked the flat and Laura knew the police would have searched it too, and so it wasn't unusual that a few items had gone missing.

Once Laura had searched the bedroom, she went out into the hallway and opened up the cupboard where they stored their coats. She went through the pockets of all of Sean's jackets, but there was nothing there. However, there was something that caught her eye. There was a panel at the back of the cupboard that looked loose. Nobody else would have noticed it, however Laura had spent hours sanding and painting those panels when they first moved in. She was a perfectionist, and she never would have left the panel like that. There had to be something behind it.

"Still nothing!" Laura called out, hoping it would stop Luke from coming to see what she was doing. With her cast sticking out at an awkward angle, she knelt and pulled up the floorboard. Laura suppressed a gasp as she saw that behind the board was a safe. Fear ran through her. Why would Sean have kept this a secret from her? She tapped away at the numbers, trying to crack the code. She tried his birthday and her birthday, but neither worked. Then she tried their anniversary and to her surprise the door swung open.

"Is it worth checking the kitchen?" Luke called, his voice sounded closer.

"Yes, please. I'll be there in a second, just grabbing a coat for myself." Laura hoped that was enough to stop him wondering what she was doing. She listened for a moment. With relief, she heard him enter the kitchen and start opening cupboards.

Turning her attention back to the safe, Laura pulled out a wedge of paperwork and stuffed it straight into the backpack, hidden beneath the clothes. To her surprise, she discovered bags of white powder behind the paperwork. Was it drugs? She didn't have time to explore any further as she heard Luke's footsteps coming towards her. Laura stuffed the drugs back in the safe, and locked it. She would find herself in more trouble if anyone found her in possession of cocaine. She then grabbed a coat from the cupboard and quickly made her way towards Luke before he became suspicious.

"Did you find anything?" she asked him, although she already knew the answer from the stoney look on his face.

"No, nothing. You?" he asked, eyeing up the bulky backpack on her back.

"No, just grabbed some new clothes for myself." she said, trying to distract his attention away from the backpack.

"What now?" he asked, running a hand through his hair. Luke looked stressed, although Laura couldn't blame him. He had probably been hoping they would stumble across clues that would lead towards them solving this, and he would be safe again.

"Why don't you just leave me here and head home? I'm sure they'll soon realise I'm no longer with you and leave you alone."

"No, I'm not leaving you." The ferocity of Luke's reply took Laura by surprise. She thought he would be happy to see the back of her.

"Sorry, I'm just stressed. I know I've only known you for a short while, Claire, but I really do care for you." A smile broke out across Luke's face and the butterflies in Laura's stomach awoke. The harsh edge had disappeared from his voice and a softness had returned to his face. She wanted to enjoy the moment and revel in someone caring about her, but there was something gnawing away at her. She just couldn't put her finger on what it was.

"Let's head back to the hotel, get a good night's sleep and come up with a new plan in the morning." Luke nodded in agreement and they both walked out of the flat, locking it behind them.

As they climbed into the lift together, Laura's brain began to piece together information. It wasn't until the lift doors shut firmly behind them, and she was trapped in a confined space, that she realised what was playing on her mind. He had called her Laura. As they walked into the flat, he had referred to her as Laura, not Claire. There was no way he could have seen her name on the post, she had scooped it up too quickly. If he had seen her name on a letter, surely he would have questioned why she had lied to him and told him she was called Claire?

Laura broke out in a cold sweat as she struggled to catch her breath. He must have known who she was all along. She was trapped in a confined space with the enemy.

CHAPTER FIFTEEN

She had to escape, but how? Running away was hardly an option with the heavy cast on her leg. With the aide of crutches she could hop away. Laura knew she would have to wait until Luke was asleep tonight and hope for the best. She wanted to scream and cry at him. He had been the first man she had trusted since Sean's death. The first man she had kissed! The first man she had been attracted to, and yet he was one of the people responsible for Sean's death. At least, he could be one of the men responsible, and that alone made Laura want to get as far away as possible from him.

"Do you need help to get into the car?" Luke asked her as they walked out of the block of flats. She did struggle with getting in and out of the car, but would not admit this to Luke. She no longer wanted any help from him.

"I'm fine, thanks." she replied, as she made her way round to the passenger side of the car. Laura kept a tight grip on the backpack that she held in her hands. As they drove back to the hotel, she hugged it close to her chest - this bag might hold some of the answers she had been looking for.

"I'm sorry, Claire. Sorry that we didn't find anything." The hairs went up on the back of Laura's neck as Luke used her false name. He was still pretending he didn't know who she was. Had he even realised that he had slipped up? Laura's mind was racing with questions as to exactly who Luke was and how he was involved in all of this. However, she knew it was unlikely she would ever get answers. Laura had to prioritise, and right now the most important thing was to get away from Luke, with the contents of the backpack. Once she found somewhere safe to stay, she could see whether her suspicions were right, and if the teddy bear held a clue.

"Would you like to talk?" It was a question that yesterday would have warmed Laura's heart. The idea that Luke cared about how she was feeling would have given her butterflies in her stomach. Today, the last thing she wanted was to talk to Luke. He reached across the car and took her hand in his. Laura had to force herself not to flinch at his touch. She couldn't let him know she had uncovered his true identity. Instead, she held her breath until he let go of her hand to steer the car around a bend.

"Perhaps tomorrow, I'm just disappointed that we didn't find anything." Laura hoped she sounded convincing, despite the tremble in her voice.

"That's fine. We'll get a good night's sleep and treat ourselves to coffees and pastries for breakfast." He shot her a dazzling smile, and yet it did nothing. All Laura could think about was how stupid she had been. The first man that had been kind to her, and she'd fallen under his spell. She had been such a fool.

They sat in silence until they arrived at the hotel when Luke offered Laura help out of the car. She refused his offer and clambered out of the car, stumbling slightly as her cast forced her off balance. She needed to remind herself what being on her own was like. If she could get away from Luke tonight, then she would be on her own for the foreseeable future with a broken ankle and crutches.

Once up in the room, Laura feigned tiredness and walked into the bathroom to get changed for bed. She still had the backpack in her hands, and she pulled out a pair of jogging bottoms and a long-sleeved top. It was just about passable as something to sleep in, but it also meant that she could sneak out of the room without getting changed. Laura desperately wanted to look at the paperwork that she had found amongst the bags of drugs, but she knew she had already been in the bathroom for too long. She folded the paperwork up and put it in the inside pocket of a pair of trousers, which she then stuffed at the bottom of the backpack, hopeful that if Luke tried to look he wouldn't find anything.

"Do you want to go straight to sleep?" Luke asked her as she re-emerged into the room. He was going out of his way to make her feel comfortable. Laura hoped his kindness wasn't because he had realised his mistake. If it were, then he might be looking for signs that she knew the truth. Laura had never been a good actress, and so she had to hope that Luke thought nothing was amiss.

"I think so. It's been a long day." Laura sighed, she really wanted to sleep, but she knew she would have to lay there, awake, waiting for her chance to escape. It was already three in the morning but thankfully being winter the sun wouldn't be up for hours yet.

"That's fine. Goodnight, Claire." Luke swiftly crossed the room and pulled her into an overly friendly hug. He had upped the physical contact since they had left the flat, and Laura suspected it was all part of hoodwinking her. She tried to relax into his embrace, but every inch of her wanted to run as far away as possible from him.

The night seemed to last forever. Laura had placed the backpack by the side of the bed and ensured that she was lying facing it, with her back towards Luke. He sat up for what seemed like forever, sending messages on his phone. Laura considered what he might be saying. He was probably reporting back on their visit to the flat. She guessed he had been hoping that she would lead him to some clues, or perhaps even to the drugs. They would be disappointed in Luke's progress, which meant Laura was in even more danger.

As Laura laid there waiting for Luke to fall asleep, she wondered what Sean would have done if it had been her that had gone missing. He would have looked for her. Or at least, she thought he would have. After having discovered the safe in their hallway cupboard and the stash of drugs, she was wondering just how well she had known her boyfriend. This was something that Laura's brain wanted to ponder, however her thoughts were interrupted as she heard someone creeping around her bed. With all the concentration she could muster, Laura focused on her breathing to mimic that of a sleeping person. This was a skill she had quickly picked up whilst sleeping rough.

Laura knew Luke was now on the side of the bed that she was facing. She heard the rustle as he picked up the backpack. Fear filled her, she didn't know what to do. She couldn't let him see the papers before she discovered what was going on. However, she also didn't want to wake up and let Luke know she was onto him. With all the restraint she could muster, Laura laid there, and pretended to be asleep, and prayed that she had hidden the letters well enough. Soon enough, she heard Luke put the backpack down beside her, and retreat to his own bed. Laura held her breath as she waited to hear the rustle of papers, but nothing came. Silence engulfed the room, and within minutes Luke was snoring softly from the other side of the room.

With the stealth of somebody with a heavy cast on their leg, Laura slipped out of bed and picked up her backpack. The room was mostly still dark, although Luke's charging phone cast a green hue around his bed. Laura crept across the room, now wishing that she had opted for the bed near the door as her crutches caused the floorboards below her to creak. Laura's heart pounded in her chest as she neared the door. Hotel doors were always so heavy and notoriously noisy, she was sure to wake Luke by opening theirs. If she hadn't had a cast on her leg, it wouldn't have worried her so much as running would have been easy. However, with a broken ankle, running was no longer an option. Laura knew she was in grave danger if she stayed with Luke and so the risk of waking him now was worth it - if there was even the slightest chance she might make it out of here alive she had to try.

She held her breath as she slowly dragged down the handle of the door. It made a slight noise, but not as loudly as Laura had been anticipating. As she opened the door, the light poured in from the hallway and so she tried to only open it enough for her to slip out. With the door shut behind her, she made her way towards the lifts, as quickly as possible. Her ribs were protesting as she pushed herself to move as fast as possible. She did not know whether

her escape had woken Luke and she didn't have time to think about it. She had to get as far away from this hotel as possible before sunrise.

Somehow, Laura was not sure how, perhaps it had been a miracle, but she made it out onto the street. She was incredibly grateful that Luke had opted to book them a city centre hotel rather than one on the outskirts of Manchester. The streets were empty, but Laura knew that several gang members must be stationed nearby. She pulled the hood up on her hoody, doing her best to hide her blonde hair and features - the less there was to recognise her by the better. The crisp early morning air whipped around her as she stumbled towards the street corner, turning into an adjacent street. Now where should she go? Laura had not thought this far ahead when she had planned her escape. She had been too focused on getting out of the hotel room. Thankfully, she knew the city well and so she kept walking, knowing that the further south she walked the closer she got to a housing estate. Not just any housing estate, the one where she grew up. Where all of her family were still living. Her hands hurt and her shoulders were in agony from the weight she was putting on them from the crutches.

As dawn broke, she walked around the familiar streets that she grew up on. There were a few early risers out for a morning jog, or walking their dog before work, however few looked her way. Laura was only a few streets from her parent's house now. She didn't know what to do, she could not put them at risk by going in, but something inside of her wanted to go home. She craved the comfort of her mother's embrace and the sweet smell of scones baking in the oven. However, those comforts would have to wait for another time, today was not the day for a family reunion. Instead, Laura crept down the side entrance of the house and let herself into the shed. Her father rarely went in the shed, only to mow the grass and fortunately it was a grey, drizzly day and so the grass was unlikely to be on the top of her father's to-do list.

CHAPTER SIXTEEN

Once inside the shed, Laura pulled out a deckchair and moved around a few items. If anyone opened the shed door, then she would be mostly hidden. It was cold, and so she grabbed the jacket that she had stowed at the top of the bag. Her eyes were stinging with tiredness and her entire body ached, especially her ankle. She wanted nothing more than to sleep and to forget about her problems, however she knew that wasn't realistic. Intrigue was pulsing adrenaline through Laura's body and instead of snuggling into the chair and falling asleep, she pulled the letters and the teddy bear from the backpack.

Laura unfolded the papers and looked down at them as her eyes adjusted to the text in front of her. She saw from the heading that they were from Sean's police force. With a deep breath to steady herself, Laura read the top letter. The teddy bear was snuggled under her arm for comfort.

Dear Mr Scott,

We are writing to inform you that The Panel met to review your recent suspension on 20th September 2019. Following your behaviour we regret to inform you we have made the decision to terminate your employment with the police force.

The severity of your behaviour and this decision by The Panel means you will no longer be eligible to apply for any future law enforcement role.

Please see the letter attached, which outlines how The Panel reached this conclusion. On this occasion we have decided not to pursue legal action.

Kind Regards,

A. Holloway

Laura's hands were shaking as she finished reading the letter. Sean had never mentioned anything to her about a suspension, and yet he had lost his job. Why had he been keeping secrets from her? Where had he been going when he had supposedly been going out to work? A million questions were floating around Laura's head, each screaming for an answer. She turned to the next page, hoping to read why The Panel reached the decision to terminate Sean's employment. Perhaps it would give her some indication as to what this 'behaviour' was.

As Laura's eyes scanned over the next letter, she realised it was not the attachment she had been hoping for. She flicked through the remaining letters, but the attached did not appear to be there. For a moment, Laura wondered whether Luke had discovered it, however she doubted he would have had enough time to go through the letters and surely she would have heard him. Accepting that the attached letter had disappeared, Laura turned her attention to the remaining papers in her hands. Each one was confirmation that Sean had the authority to work undercover. Laura was no stranger to seeing these letters, as Sean often did undercover work. She also knew that the letters would not give any information on what the undercover operation was about. With a frustrated sigh, she stuffed the letters into a drawer in the shed. So far, she had only become more confused about the situation.

Sean had obviously been working undercover, however it looked as though something had gone very wrong. He had done something that had led to him losing his job and almost resulted in legal proceedings. Something so bad that he could not confide in her. Laura closed her eyes and prepared herself for looking at the teddy bear. It was her last chance. Once she had explored this potential clue, she didn't know what to do next. Her hands were still trembling as she opened her eyes and held the teddy bear up to the light. Where was the clue? It took her a few minutes of inspecting the bear before she realised that the back seam looked as though somebody had re-stitched it. Surely not, she thought to herself. Sean must have been desperate to hide whatever was in this bear. On the workbench to her left there was a Stanley knife, and Laura reached out to use it to unpick the seams. She didn't want to ruin the teddy bear. As silly as it sounded, it was a symbol of a happy memory that they had shared.

Once the stitches had been unpicked, Laura pulled out some stuffing when her fingers brushed against paper. A sick feeling washed over Laura as she pulled the hidden letter from inside the bear. Her hands were clammy as she straightened out the piece of paper. What on earth had been going on for Sean to hide these words? Laura recognised Sean's handwriting on the paper. He usually typed everything, and so he must have been avoiding any trace of this letter. Laura prepared herself to read his words. She knew her heart would break all over again as she imagined him sat at their desk writing this.

◆ ◆ ◆

My Dearest Laura,

If you're reading this, then I am truly sorry. Something must have gone wrong. Very, very wrong. My work means that I have to keep so much from you. When you think I'm just popping out to the station for my evening shift, or patrolling the streets, I'm often lying to you. Lately, my work has heavily revolved around a highly secretive undercover operation. So secretive that nobody at my station even knows about it.

I want to tell you everything, but I don't know whether I should. I need you to be safe. Laura, never forget how much I have loved and always will love you. Everything I do is to keep you safe and to make you happy. This undercover operation will be my last, I know it's too dangerous to keep doing this.

After all these years, I know you well enough to know that by now you'll be screaming at this piece of paper, urging me to just get on with it and tell you exactly what is going on. I suspect that if you're reading this letter, things will be so bad that you have a right to know what is going on, so here goes...

I'm working undercover in one of the biggest drug operations in existence. However, things have turned sour. I promise you, Laura, that whatever anyone says, I have not gone rogue. The police don't believe me, and I've gone deeper into the operation than I really should have. I've done things I'm not proud of, but I promise you I'm doing it for the right reasons.

If anything happens to me, then please protect yourself. I've tried to cover my tracks but I can't guarantee your safety and that scares the living hell out of me. I'll always be there to protect you, even if you think I've gone.

Love always,

Sean

Laura had to move the note away to stop her tears from erasing the words. It was just as she had suspected, Sean had been working undercover. However, it looked as though the organised crime group had discovered what he was doing. With every ounce of self-control left inside her, Laura took a deep breath to stop herself from dissolving into uncontrollable sobs. Reading Sean's letter had brought back a plethora of emotions. She loved him and missed him so incredibly much. As she re-read the last line of the letter, Laura couldn't help but wonder why Sean had chosen those words. What did he mean when he said he would be there to protect her, even if she thought he was gone? The familiar feeling of hope tried to rise within her, but she swiftly quashed it. She knew the pain would be unbearable if she allowed herself to consider the possibility of Sean still being alive.

By now, Laura's eyes were protesting, and she knew she couldn't force herself to stay awake any longer. There were still so many unanswered questions in her head, but she knew she would not be getting any answers anytime soon. Instead, she wiped her eyes and allowed herself to drift off to sleep, somewhat comforted knowing that her family were only across the garden.

CHAPTER SEVENTEEN

When Laura woke, she was grateful to see that the sun was setting outside. She was shivering sat inside her family's shed but she knew she would have to wait until it was dark outside to move. Her stomach was screaming at her to find some food, but she didn't have time to think about that right now. Laura had to decide where she would be safe whilst she figured out what to do next. She longed to walk into a police station, find a kind-looking officer, and seek safety and protection from them. However, Laura had watched Sean's career in the police force for long enough to know that even there she wouldn't be safe. An organised crime group like the one that was after her would have many corrupt officers. Perfectly situated to capture her and bring them to her under the false pretences of keeping her safe.

There was nobody Laura could turn to right now. Her family were mere feet away from her and yet she had to leave them - she had to do this alone. Laura knew she couldn't lose herself in her thoughts, and so she took a deep breath and stood up to stretch her legs, her head banging the shed ceiling above. She had to think about where to go next, and she had to think fast. By now, they would be out looking for her, waiting for her to make an appearance. With a last glance at Sean's handwriting, she hid the letter in the shed behind her dad's toolbox. If they caught her, she didn't want them to read his last words to her. Once she had hidden all the paperwork, she pulled on another layer of clothes. By now it was dark outside and Laura knew she had to take this opportunity to leave. Her father kept a jar of change in the shed, and so Laura grabbed the jar and stashed it in her backpack. She had a plan. Hopefully, there would be enough change to buy her a coach ticket. She didn't care where the coach took her. Anywhere away from here would be okay. She needed somewhere to hide while she decided what to do next. The first step was to get as far away as possible from her family. She had already put them in danger by coming here.

With her decision fresh in her mind, Laura silently exited the shed and made her way down the side of the house. She was too afraid to even breathe in case anyone discovered her. Once out on the street, with her hood pulled up to disguise her face, she was free. All she needed to do was lie-low until her ankle had healed and then she could take more risks and properly look for Sean. A sense of excitement came over her. She had a plan, and there was even the chance that Sean might still be alive somewhere.

Before Laura could get too carried away with her thoughts, she heard a van behind her, slowing down as it approached. She wanted to pick up her feet and run as far away as she could, but it was impossible. Before she could even piece together a plan, the side of the van had swung open and a masked man jumped out. His hand immediately went across her mouth to muffle any noise that tried to escape her. Fear engulfed every one of Laura's senses as they bundled her into the back of the van. Her eyes bulged with horror before they slammed the door shut and she succumbed to the darkness around her. Laura could feel the van moving beneath her as she tried to steady herself. The man who had grabbed her still had his hand across her mouth, whilst his hot breath tickled her neck. Laura wanted to recoil as far away as possible from the man, however someone else's arm was wrapped firmly around her stomach, keeping her anchored in place.

A light shining directly into her eyes blinded Laura. She tried to retreat from it, but the man holding her in place wouldn't allow her to move even an inch.

"Tie her up, quick!" A gruff voice from across the van shouted. They sounded impatient. Laura tried to scream, but the hand around her mouth only clamped down harder. Instead, she tried to kick and punch, but before she could land a blow, the men held her down. They tied her legs and her wrists together. They must have been using rope. It was tight and rough against her skin, the pain was searing but Laura knew she had to be brave. Whether she made it out of this situation, or not, she would do everything she could to protect Sean and not give any information away.

The bright light that had been shone in her eyes was a torch that they were now using to see as they tied her up. It took a few moments for Laura's eyes to adjust, but in the dim light she could see that she was in the back of a van, surrounded by four masked men. Laura's eyes fell on the fourth man who was sitting by the side of the van and not partaking in tying her up. He looked just the same as the others, wearing the uniform, however he had one thing that distinguished him from those tying her up. He had a gun. Despite the dim lighting, there was no mistaking that the object in this man's hand was a gun and it was pointing right at her. Laura tried to shrink away from him as her body trembled.

Struggling to regulate her heart rate, Laura was pulled up into a seated position where a piece of tape was roughly stuck across her mouth. Her entire body was in pain. She couldn't have screamed, even if she had wanted to. Her mind was too busy focusing on the gun that was pointing directly at her. With just a flex of his finger, the man sat opposite could kill her. Laura wondered what it would be like for everything to end here, in the back of this van. Despite wanting to find out what happened to Sean, she was exhausted. Perhaps it wouldn't be so bad if they shot her. At least she could finally stop prowling the streets for somewhere to sleep every night.

"Five minutes!" A voice came from the front of the van. The men surrounding her didn't make a sound to acknowledge that they had heard the warning. Laura couldn't help but wonder what five minutes meant. Five minutes until they shot her, or five minutes until they arrived at their destination? Perhaps both had the same outcome.

Those five minutes seemed to last forever as the van bounced up and down over potholes. With her arms and legs bound, Laura was reliant on the two men either side of her to keep her upright, however neither of them had much regard for her comfort. This wasn't how she had ever envisioned her death. Like many, she had hoped that old age would eventually steal her away in her sleep.

The man was still pointing the gun at her, the dim light reflecting off of the barrel, a constant reminder of the danger she was in. Closing her eyes, Laura tried to imagine Sean's arms around her, telling her that everything would be okay. It had been so long since he had held her; it was almost impossible to recall the feeling.

"How are we going to get her to the room?" The man holding the gun broke the silence, forcing Laura to open her eyes and confront the situation she was in.

"We could carry her?" The man to the left suggested. Laura noticed that neither of the men had a distinct accent. She suspected it was all part of their training to be a gang member. Nothing about them could single them out, they had to all look and act alike.

"Just undo her legs but keep a hold of her. She won't go far with that cast on her." With the order given, the men reached into their pockets and each pulled out a penknife before cutting the ropes that bound her. The more Laura witnessed, the more scared she became. These men knew what they were doing, she couldn't rely on them making mistakes to escape. She cursed the cast on her leg. If she hadn't been so foolish that day then none of this would have happened - she never would have met Luke. Or perhaps she was always going to meet Luke? After all, he had been at the homeless shelter. She thought she had remembered seeing him before the bus hit her. He had been tracking her before she arrived at the hospital. As Laura thought back to that day, she remembered how tired she had been leaving the shelter. Luke had drugged her. Anger clouded her vision as she conjured up Luke's face in her mind. How could he have been so cruel and heartless?

As the van came to a halt, they threw open the doors, and to Laura's disappointment it was pitch black outside. She had hoped that wherever they had driven to would be somewhere she recognised. With some difficulty and a lot of pain, the two men pushed Laura towards the door and out of the van. She landed on her feet with such a jolt that it sent pain through her broken ankle, making her cry out around the tape that was still covering her mouth. Laura bit down on her tongue, trying to ignore the searing pain in her ankle, as they immediately forced her to walk. Two of the men stood on either side of her, helping her to walk since they had left her crutches by the side of the road as they bundled her into the van. She forced herself to concentrate on her surroundings, rather than the pain. She would need to remember the route they took if she ever stood a chance of escaping.

Although it was dark outside, the moon was out, casting a waxy glow over everything. Laura could just about decipher that they were in a carpark of what appeared to be an industrial estate. They were walking towards a warehouse which looked like nobody had stepped foot inside for decades. There were shattered windows and boarded up doors. It didn't look like a place anyone ever went, which meant that Laura couldn't comfort herself in thinking people might find her in the morning. She wondered whether this was where they had brought Sean. Perhaps he had died before he had even left the flat. Laura had to shake her head to stop her thoughts running away with themselves. She had to be completely in control of herself. Her life, and possibly Sean's, depended on it.

They walked through one of the open doorways. The door had been smashed in some time ago. Laura shivered as the cold air enveloped her and the hairs on the back of her neck stood up. The man with the gun was standing behind her and she didn't have to turn around to know that it was millimetres from her back. Unshed tears filled her eyes, making it almost impossible to see where she was going. With her eyesight compromised, her other senses heightened and a sudden overwhelming smell of damp hit her. She dreaded to think what she was walking over as the debris crunched beneath her. It was dark, but the man at the front and the man at the back each had a torch, casting an orange glow. They followed a maze of hallways. Laura tried to make a mental note of where they turned and how many flights of stairs they climbed, but it was impossible. Each corridor was the same, dark, smashed in windows, broken lights hanging from ceilings, and now and then the sound of rats scurrying around would break the silence. Laura's hands shook behind her as the rope continued to rub against her skin. She could feel the wounds opening on her wrists.

Eventually, they walked into a large room, where they had placed a chair in the middle. The windows to the room were all situated up high, close to the ceiling. It reminded Laura of a public swimming pool. Moonlight flooded in from the windows. Before Laura could take in the rest of her surroundings, the men shoved her into the seat and quickly tied her to it. Laura could see the shadow of someone walking through a set of doors at the back of the hallway. Dread filled her as she recognised the silhouette.

"Why didn't you just stay at the hotel with me, Claire? Or should I call you Laura? Which do you prefer?" Luke walked towards her as someone flicked on the overhead lights. In the harsh artificial light, she looked into his face and wondered how she had ever been attracted to him. Perhaps it was because she now knew what was behind that sickly sweet smile. The inquisitive eyes that once drew her in now repulsed her. He continued to walk towards her, until he was standing over her, leering down at her. In one swift motion, he tore the tape away from Laura's mouth. She winced in pain. It had been a while since she'd had her top lip waxed.

"What do you want?" She spat at him. He was the last person she wanted to see. The men surrounding her were armed, and yet they didn't scare her as much as Luke did. He was the real animal here - completely lacking a heart. He had listened to her cry, been a shoulder to cry on, encouraged her to trust him and had even tried to seduce her, and yet here he was about to kill her.

"Do you not want to ask some more exciting questions? Perhaps like how we knew where you were?" The smile on Luke's face was smug as he knelt down in front of her, forcing her to make eye contact with him.

"I don't care." She shrugged her shoulders and forced her face to appear blank. Of course she wanted to know how they had found her, but she wouldn't let him see that. The last thing she wanted was to show Luke any sign of weakness.

"I put a tracker in that backpack of yours. Although we didn't know what house you were in so we had to be patient until you reappeared." Luke laughed. It was a horrible noise. If Laura had been able to move her arms, she would have placed her hands over her ears to block out the sound. Laura breathed a sigh of relief. They didn't seem to know that she had been at her parent's house.

With the mention of her backpack, one of the men came forward and thrust it into Luke's grip. Laura breathed a sigh of relief that she had thought ahead enough to hide the letters. The only thing left in the backpack were clothes and a framed picture of herself and Sean. She'd even left the teddy behind in the shed. Luke turned the backpack upside down, allowing its contents to tumble out onto the concrete floor. The picture hit the ground and Laura winced as she heard the glass shatter.

"Oh bless, she took a picture of her pig of a boyfriend. He wasn't a very good police officer. It was quite entertaining that his cover was blown by one of his own. Shame we had to kill the informant." Luke let out a dark chuckle as he picked up the broken frame and threw it to the other side of the room. Laura cringed as she thought about how much she had once loved that frame. She would look at the picture every night before going to sleep. Life was different now though, Sean wasn't here. She had to forget about such a sentimental thing. She watched as Luke rooted through the pile of clothes on the floor. He was so sure he was going to find something. Despite the fear and pain, Laura couldn't help but feel a little bubble of smugness rise within her - he wouldn't find a thing.

"Where is it?" he shouted at her, his face millimetres from hers. Laura refused to flinch, instead she kept staring directly at him as she replied.

"Where's what?" she asked, her tone of voice as sickly sweet as she could manage.

"Whatever you found in the flat," he shouted at her again,

spit spraying her face as a vein in his forehead throbbed. He was fuming.

"I didn't find anything." She shrugged her shoulders, enjoying seeing him getting so wound up. There was no way Luke was the mastermind behind all of this, he was just one of someone else's minions and the longer he went without any success the more trouble he would be in.

"Liar!" he screamed back at her. Before Laura could brace herself for what was to come, he lifted his hand and swung it. The thump echoed throughout the room as his fist connected with her head. Laura lost consciousness before she could even scream out in pain.

CHAPTER EIGHTEEN

When Laura regained consciousness, it was light outside. She could hear birds singing through the broken windows. Whilst she was grateful for the light, the sound of birds and little else emphasised the remote location. She moved her head to see who was in the room with her, but a piercing pain resounded throughout her skull. Her head was pounding and her vision still a little blurry from when Luke had hit her.

"She's awake." Laura recognised the voice from the previous evening. It was one of the men who had been in the van with her. She turned her head to where the noise had come from, trying to ignore the pain. The man had been speaking into a phone, but he quickly shut off the call and put the phone back into his pocket. The phone was identical to the one Luke had given her. Thankfully, she had left it behind at his flat in London. The man still had the gun clutched in his hands. Perhaps he was afraid she might try to fight back. Unfortunately, the most Laura could do in a fight was to trip someone up with her cast.

A few minutes later, footsteps echoed down the hallway. They were coming towards the room. Laura took a deep breath, steeling herself for whatever was to come next.

She didn't care how much pain they put her through, she would do everything she could to protect Sean, just in case he had somehow escaped. Laura's heart sunk as she watched Luke walk back into the room. He was the last person she ever wanted to see.

"I see you've finally decided to wake up." His snide remark made the anger inside her boil, but Laura knew not to rise to it. She had to be the adult here. Instead of replying, she just watched him as he grabbed a chair and came to sit in front of her, leaving a few feet in between them.

"We have some things we need to talk about." Laura's insides churned as she watched his mouth move and she thought about how she had kissed his lips. What had she been thinking? Perhaps he had drugged her to make her susceptible to falling for him.

"Shall we play twenty questions then? I'll go first. Why are you such an arsehole?" Although Laura had promised to be the adult, she couldn't help herself. Sometimes she had no control over her mouth, especially when she had kissed the brute sat in front of her.

"I think that sense of humour is probably why Sean left you for dead." Luke knew his statement would send her mind racing. Sean would never have left her for dead. She had to control her thoughts - Luke was good - he knew which buttons to press and she had to avoid walking into his trap. She had opened her soul to him, told him of her heartbreak, and he would try to use all of that against her.

"Shall we count that as your first question?" she quipped back, not missing a beat. She would not show Luke any

119

sign of weakness.

"I like it when you're feisty." Laura had to stop herself from gagging as he leaned forward and placed his hand on her knee. His touch, that once gave her butterflies, now made her sick to her stomach.

"Two questions down. Do we get to stop for a coffee break halfway through?" As the words slipped out, Laura almost regretted asking as it reminded her of the hunger eating away at her insides. She couldn't remember the last time she had eaten.

"Where are the drugs, Laura?" Luke's playful manner had disappeared almost immediately, his face stoney as he retracted his touch.

"What drugs?" Laura asked, her mind flitting back to the safe inside their hallway cupboard. Surely all this wasn't over a few bags of cocaine?

"You know exactly what drugs." Luke stood up from his chair and closed the distance between them until he was kneeling down in front of her again.

"What drugs?" Laura repeated the question. Despite Luke's anger, she also wanted answers, and it seemed that this entire situation revolved around these drugs.

"The drugs that your stupid boyfriend stole from us!" He was shouting in her face again, but Laura barely noticed, she was too busy focusing on the words he was saying. Why would Sean have stolen drugs from an organised crime group? Laura lacked the years of police training that Sean had, but even she knew that stealing drugs was like signing your own death warrant, whilst also obliterating your career. Perhaps that was what the letter of termination had been about. Had Sean stolen these drugs? Laura suddenly wondered if the drugs were the reason behind Sean's erratic behaviour over their last few months together. Surely he wasn't stupid enough to have used the drugs.

"You spent so long trying to get me to trust you. I told you everything I know." It was almost true. During her time spent with Luke, she had told him everything she knew. However, since escaping from him she had learned more about what was going on - he didn't need to know that though.

"I don't believe it. That's okay though, we don't need your information. We just need you." The smirk had returned to Luke's face. A chill ran down Laura's spine - they obviously had a plan.

"What am I supposed to do?" she asked, thankful that Luke had retreated to his seat again.

"Oh, you don't have to do anything. We just need you to stay sat there. Once message gets to Sean, he won't be able to help himself, he'll have to come and save you. Well, at least we hope so. I hope you haven't been lying to me about how much he loves you."

The room spun around Laura. What did they mean? Could it really be true? Was Sean really still alive? Luke laughed as he watched the turmoil on Laura's face.

"Oh. yes, sorry. Did I forget to tell you? Sean's alive." He stood up to leave.

"Wait! How is he alive?" Laura shouted. She couldn't just

let him leave without getting any answers.

"He was shot at the flat, but somehow he got away. Over a year now we've been trying to find him. We don't know where he is, but we've got connections that can try to get a message to him." With that, Luke left the room, ordering one of the men to get some food for Laura.

The room continued to spin as Laura tried to make sense of what she had just been told. She couldn't help but wonder if Luke was right. Surely Sean would have found her if he was still alive? He must have known that she would be vulnerable on her own and that the group would target her to get to him? He was either dead or he didn't love her. Either way, Laura couldn't imagine any explanation that would result in Sean turning up to save her.

"Eat!" One of the men shoved a smoothie into her hands. It was shop bought and sickly sweet looking, but it was probably just what Laura needed. She allowed the man to bring the bottle to her lips and tipped her head backwards so she could drink. If she could satisfy the hunger pains she was feeling, then perhaps she could organise her thoughts enough to figure out how she could get out of this situation alive. If that was even possible.

Laura didn't stop for breath until she had finished every drop of the smoothie. It was strawberry and banana, her favourite. She wondered whether Luke had remembered a late night conversation they'd had one evening about their favourite food and drinks. It was hard to imagine this Luke was the same man as the one who had cared for her in London. As Laura tried to fight the memories, she realised her vision was blurring again and her thoughts were becoming harder and harder to hold on to. She fought to hold on to her consciousness, but it didn't do any good. They had drugged the smoothie.

CHAPTER NINETEEN

When Laura next regained consciousness, it was dark outside. She didn't know how long she had been unconscious for, it could have been hours or it could have been days. Her entire body hurt from sitting and sleeping on a wooden chair. She vaguely remembered them rousing her to use the toilet. Her memory was hazy, but they had shoved her towards a corner where a curtain and a bucket were situated. Laura was thankful for the drugs in her system as she didn't recall what had happened next. She scanned her body, checking for any further injuries, however she didn't find any. Her ankle was enjoying the rest. Laura's mind was foggy from the cocktail of drugs that they had been plying her with. Although it was dark in the room, she could sense several other people there with her, most likely watching her. Laura concentrated on regulating her breathing and kept her head hanging so that it looked like she was still asleep. As soon as they realised, she was awake they would try to drug her again and right now she had too much to think about to risk losing consciousness again.

Sean was alive. That was something Laura was still trying to get her head around. Deep down, she knew it had always been a possibility. After all, there was no body, he had only been presumed dead. Despite this, she had always assumed that if he had been alive, he would have tried to find her, even if that meant being found. He always said he would do anything for her, and yet he had left her fighting for her life for over a year now. Laura was slowly realising that perhaps she didn't know Sean as well as she had thought.

"Still no sign of your beloved boyfriend." A chill ran down Laura's spine. How could the sound of a voice provoke such a response? Especially a voice that had once captivated all of her senses. She refused to give Luke the satisfaction of an answer, instead she remained sitting there with her head positioned towards her lap.

"Perhaps we should start harming you. Maybe that will encourage him to come and save you?" Luke's voice was full of venom, he was obviously under a lot of pressure from someone higher up the chain. He was unrecognisable from the man she first met.

Laura was bursting with questions, but she refused to give Luke the satisfaction. Somehow, she still had some control over herself. She heard his footsteps echoing throughout the room as he came closer to her.

"Come on Laura, don't ignore me." He crouched down in front of her and pulled her chin up to look at him. Every inch of Laura recoiled from his touch against her face.

"What more do you want from me?" she hissed back at him.

"I just need to use you as bait for Sean." He shrugged his shoulders, refusing to let go of her face.

"Why don't we play another game of twenty questions whilst we wait?" she asked him. Laura didn't think she would get any real answers, but she wanted to play for time - she needed enough time for the drugs to clear from her system so that she could form a plan.

"I suppose it might pass some time." Luke conceded and motioned for someone to bring him a chair. Laura breathed a sigh of relief as his hands left her face. She only wished she could erase the memory of his touch.

"I'll go first." Laura was feeling bold. After all, what more could they do to her? She'd been through hell already. "Why did you save me at the hospital? Surely it would have been easier for them to just kidnap me then."

"Good question." Luke nodded in admiration as he sat down on his chair and made himself comfortable. He was enjoying having the upper hand and forcing Laura to wait for his answer. "Unfortunately, the idiots that paid you a visit in the hospital were a little heavy-handed. They would have killed you had I not stepped in. As fun as it would have been to watch them slowly kill you, we need you to lure Sean to us."

Laura hadn't expected the answer to be so sinister. Every aspect of this had been plotted, all leading up to this moment.

"So it wasn't a coincidence that you met me at the shelter?" Laura was finding it difficult to piece together all the information. How long had Luke been following her, just waiting for the perfect moment to fool her?

"No, now that was a coincidence. We knew you were in

London and so a few of us were deployed to homeless shelters to see if we could find you. Imagine my joy when you stumbled into *my* shelter. I drugged your dinner, which is why you were so out of it the following day and then you were hit by the bus. It wasn't luck that led you to my hospital, it was all planned." The smile on Luke's face further repulsed Laura. He was ruthless, he had carefully calculated every word and every one of his actions to lure her in.

"You're disgusting!" Laura screamed at the top of her lungs, the sound echoed throughout the building.

"Oh, come on, Laura, you didn't always think I was disgusting." Luke wiggled his eyebrows at her and she heard a chorus of cheers from the thugs standing guard. Laura took a deep breath to stop herself from responding. She had to focus on finding a way out of this. As time passed, she knew Sean wasn't coming for her. If he had known that she was in such danger, he would have been there straight away. She would have to fight for her own life.

"Luke, can you have a look at my ribs for me, I think there's swelling there?" Laura steeled herself for his touch. The last thing she wanted was for him to come anywhere near her, but it was necessary for her plan to work. She only hoped that she had read the situation right and that Luke really was the one in charge here. Whilst she had been asking him questions, she had loosened the ropes around her wrists. Her legs were already free. When tying her to the chair, they hadn't seen the point in tying her legs because of her cast. Once she shed the ropes around her wrists, she would be free.

Luke towered over her and pulled her top up so that he

could see her ribs. She couldn't think about that though, she had to be quick because she'd only get one chance. As the ropes slid from her arms, she lunged forward for the gun that was attached to Luke's belt.

"Help!" he shouted, immediately knowing what she was trying to do.

Laura's fingertips touched the cool metal of the gun. The sound of a gunshot resounded throughout the room. Fear filled Laura and time stilled. It was as if she could see the bullet flying through the air, it was coming right at her and there was nothing she could do to avoid it.

CHAPTER TWENTY

Sean Scott

27 October 2019

The sound of a gunshot ricocheted throughout the living room as a blistering pain radiated down Sean Scott's side. He fell to his knees from the shock of the pain. Despite his injuries, he couldn't help but think how annoyed his girlfriend, Laura, would be at him bleeding on their new carpet. With a tremendous amount of courage, he looked down to see where he had been wounded. It looked to be his arm, however there was a lot of blood.

"Let's get him in the van." One of the men surrounding him suggested. The others agreed and before Sean knew what was happening, they had pressed a jacket against his wound, so nobody would notice it, before they dragged him towards the door. Sean tried to focus on what was happening, rather than the pain he was in. However, it was proving to be difficult.

Sean had a man on either side of him, pulling him along. His legs were trying to keep up, but he he was growing weaker from the blood loss. Somehow, the men got him into the lift and downstairs to an awaiting van. Sean knew that if he got into the van, he would be dead by the end of the day. With all the strength he had left in him, he spun around, throwing the men off of him in surprise. He had a fraction of a second to make the right decision. If he took the wrong turn and one of the men caught him, he would be dead. He sprinted to his left, quickly turning the corner as he heard the footsteps of the men close behind him. The pain was making it almost impossible for Sean to see where he was going, but with all the adrenaline of someone running for their life, he pushed on. Suddenly, a car pulled up beside him and Sean breathed a sigh of relief as its occupants pulled him in.

"They know who you are." His supervisor commented as the driver sped off. Sean had barely caught his breath when he was thrown back into the seat at the speed the car was going.

"I noticed." Sean eventually spat back. It was their fault his cover had been blown.

"Let's get you to a doctor before we decide what our next course of action will be."

They sat in silence as the car weaved in and out of the traffic. The drive seemed to go on for hours as Sean drifted in and out of consciousness. At long last, they pulled up outside an unsuspecting building. To the untrained eye, it looked like a disused office block. However, Sean knew that within those walls lay a secret warren of top tier police officers and their support staff. As the car came to a stop, two burly looking security guards walked out of the doorway, and checked their identities via fingerprint before allowing them into the building. Two officers, who had been in the car, escorted Sean to the doctor with the promise of a debrief once the doctor was satisfied that he was okay.

Sean couldn't recall much of his time in the doctor's office. The pain was now excruciating, and he was slipping in and out of consciousness. When he eventually came round again, he was lying on the examination table with an IV drip in his hand. The doctor was sitting at his desk waiting for him to wake.

"Ah, Mr Scott, you're awake." He immediately noticed Sean's small movements, and he made his way over to him.

"How long have I been out for?" Sean asked, feeling rather groggy as he tried to recall the events that had led to him ending up here.

"Only an hour or two. You're lucky, the bullet just missed anything vital. I've removed it and patched you up, but you will have to keep redressing the wound and you'll have a scar." At the mention of a bullet the events all came flooding back to Sean, he sat up quickly only for the world to start spinning around him.

"I need to go. Laura will be home from work soon." He couldn't risk leaving her on her own. The gang would be looking for her. Who knew what they would do to her? Sean couldn't even bear to let his mind ponder the possibilities. He had to be with her.

"Sorry, sir, but I'm under strict instructions not to let you leave my office. They have locked us in."

"I'll break the door down, stand aside." Sean commanded the doctor, however the doctor refused to move.

"With all due respect, sir, I cannot move and even if I wanted to, I highly doubt you have the energy to break down a door after everything that has happened to you today." The doctor's voice was filled with compassion, but there was a steeliness underneath that Sean knew would be impossible to penetrate. He was imprisoned in this room until one of his superiors came and spoke to him.

Thankfully, the wait was brief and after a few minutes Sean's supervisor unlocked the door, strolled in and locked the door behind him. He knew Sean far too well.

"Sean, it's good to see you looking better." The man pulled up a chair next to his bed, whilst the doctor retreated to his desk to pretend he couldn't hear the conversation that was about to take place.

"Let me out, please. I have to make sure Laura is okay." Sean pleaded, he poured all of his emotions into that one sentence. He knew he would only get the one chance to ask and so he had to ensure he made it clear how important it was.

"Sean, relax, please. There's an officer stationed at the flat. They will ensure that Laura is okay and once we've extracted her from the scene, we'll place her in protective custody." Sean mulled over his supervisor's words. With an officer stationed at the flat, Laura would be okay. They could soon be together, although she would probably lecture him on the danger that he had put them both in. A small smile spread across his lips as he thought of her face, scrunching up in anger as she reprimanded him.

"What happened?" Sean asked, he knew that one of the other undercover officers had blown his cover. The gang had told him. They knew everything about his undercover operation and about him being the one who stole the drugs.

"The recruit told them everything. At least, we think so. We recovered his body this morning."

Sean lashed out and knocked over a chair. It was their fault that all this had happened. One of their stupid undercover officers had blown his cover. Sean had told his supervisor that the boy was not ready for an under-cover operation, but nobody had listened to him. Now, a week after the boy had joined, they had murdered him and he had told the gang everything. Sean was lucky to be alive, and he knew the gang would be after him. He also knew that they wouldn't think twice about using Laura for leverage - he had to make sure she was safe. Sean took a deep breath to control the anger that was simmering away.

"What's happening now?" Sean knew he couldn't go home, nor could he rejoin the investigation.

"You'll also go into protective care. Sean, I'm sure you don't need me to tell you how much danger you are in. This gang will do whatever they can to silence you, espe-cially since you have extensive knowledge of their oper-ations. Not to mention the stash of drugs that you stole."

Sean cringed at the memory of stealing the cocaine. There had been many deaths in the area linked to a bad batch of drugs. The undercover operation had required Sean to take a sample of the drugs so that they could connect the gang to the deaths. That weekend Sean had snuck into the warehouse to steal a sample of the drugs, however he couldn't bear the thought of any more innocent people losing their lives and so he had loaded all five kilos into the back of a hire car. On Monday morning, when the gang leader, known as H, arrived at the warehouse and discovered that almost four hundred thousand pounds' worth of drugs were missing, he had been fuming. His supervisor was right, Sean would have a price on his head and anyone who killed him would be commended.

"Okay. When are we doing this?" Sean knew he didn't really have a choice in the matter. He just wanted to get to safety so that Laura could join him. They would have to go into hiding until they prosecuted the gang, and then they would most likely have to relocate. It would be okay though, because they would be together.

"You'll leave tomorrow. We will report yourself and Laura as missing. We don't want the gang to know that you're under police custody." His supervisor gave him a last nod before leaving. Sean thought about how worried his and Laura's families would be. He was causing people insurmountable pain because of his job.

A few minutes later, somebody else came into the room to show Sean to a room for the night. The doctor promised he would be along shortly to check Sean's wound.

CHAPTER
TWENTY ONE

Sean barely slept that night and when he did, nightmares of the gang catching Laura filled his head. He had to keep reminding himself that she was safe. He knew his colleagues were capable. The pain medications were all wearing off and the dull throb in his arm was only making sleep harder. Sean breathed a sigh of relief as day broke outside. The room he was staying in was not much different to a cell and he suspected that if he tried the door, he would find it locked. He was now in protective custody, which meant that he was at their mercy. All these years working for the police force, and this was what it had come to. He knew that after this undercover operation finished, it would be highly unlikely he could continue with his job. Perhaps he could get Laura to teach him how to cook. Although that hadn't ended too well the last time he had tried. They had made a deal - she would help him learn how to cook, meanwhile he would teach her how to shoot. The shooting lesson had ended in a trip to A&E.

23rd December 2016,

"Do I need anything else?" Laura emerged from the bedroom wearing camouflage trousers, t-shirt and hoodie. Sean had to stop himself from laughing at her appearance.

"Who said that?" he joked, pretending he couldn't see her standing in front of him. Laura rolled her eyes at his terrible joke and grabbed a coat from the cupboard. It was a drizzly December day, but she was insistent that they did not cancel their lesson.

Sean had packed one of his air rifles so that Laura could learn to shoot with pellets, before moving onto bullets. He was a little apprehensive about teaching her how to shoot, but he knew it would be beneficial for her to learn how to protect herself. Sean hated that his work meant that he was putting Laura's safety in jeopardy.

"You can drive." Laura threw the car keys at Sean after locking the front door to their flat. Sean caught them with ease and followed Laura to the car. One of their friends owned a farm and had offered one of their fields for Laura's lesson. Sean had taken the time to ensure that the field was not near any livestock - he wasn't sure how good Laura's aim would be. Earlier in the week, Sean had visited the farm and set out some hay bales for target practise.

The drive to the farm didn't take them long and after a short walk they arrived at the field that Sean had set-up.

"You ready?" Sean asked, glancing over at Laura. She was biting her bottom lip, and he had to fight the urge to wrap her in his arms and kiss her. He couldn't risk thoughts like that distracting him, not when he was about to let Laura loose with an air rifle.

"Perhaps this is a bad idea." Laura glanced nervously at the rifle as Sean pulled it from its case. It had been a present to him from his parents when he started working with the police.

"You'll be fine! Besides, if anything goes wrong you're dressed in camouflage so nobody will even know you were here." Sean did his best to lighten the mood. He enjoyed learning to shoot with his father, and he wanted Laura to enjoy it too.

"Okay, talk me through it. Then repeat it all over again so you're sure I understand it." It wasn't often that Laura was unsure of herself, but in this instant her confidence had dropped and Sean wanted to do everything in his power to prove to her she could do this. He slowly talked her through how the gun worked and the science behind each element. Once he was sure she understood, he demonstrated aiming and shooting the gun. Laura watched in awe and tried not to be distracted by how attractive Sean looked shooting a gun.

"It's your turn to have a go." Sean held the rifle out for Laura to take. Her hands shook as she took the object into her grasp. He helped her wrap her hands around the gun and position it against her shoulder so that she could align the shot. Sean stood back and held his breath as Laura adjusted her aim for the closest hay bale. She took a deep breath before pulling the trigger. Time stood still as the pellet flew through the air. Neither Sean, nor Laura, could breathe as they waited to see whether she would hit the target. Laura let out a squeal as the pellet hit the hay bale. Sean wrapped his arms around her waist, spinning her around as they both laughed. He was so proud of her.

"Try again, just in case that was beginner's luck." Sean teased

her as he finally pulled his lips away from hers. He had to remind himself again not to become distracted. This time Sean stood next to Laura and watched as she aimed the gun. Before Sean could react, two things happened - a stray sheep wandered into the field, making Laura jump as she pulled the trigger. The gun fell from her hands as it discharged the pellet. It took a few seconds for it to sink in and as it did Sean staggered, falling to the floor. Laura had shot him in the foot.

"Oh my god, are you okay?" Laura screamed, kneeling down beside him.

"You just shot me in the foot!" he screamed back, annoyed that she had asked such a stupid question when he was visibly in pain. "Take my shoe off, but be careful." Laura did as she was told and carefully prised his shoe from his foot. The trainer had a small-pellet-sized-hole at the top of it. Sean berated himself for not wearing proper footwear. He could have avoided this. His sock had a similar hole in it, and blood was soaking the surrounding area.

"I think it's just a flesh wound." Laura commented, inspecting his foot.

"There's a first aid kit in the car, let's bandage it and then you can drive me to A&E." Laura helped Sean to the car and then went back to get the gun and his discarded sock and shoe. Thankfully, working in a kitchen, Laura had some basic first aid training and so she gave the wound a quick clean and bandaged it.

Five hours they spent in A&E to be told that it was only a flesh wound. They were discharged with fresh bandages and a warning to be more careful shooting guns.

After some persuasion, Laura agreed to try again. Thankfully, her aim greatly improved. They sometimes had a date night at the firing range in Manchester, followed by dinner and drinks; always in that order, Sean didn't want to risk being shot, again. The door to Sean's room opened with a loud creak, pulling him from his reminiscing. Standing in the doorway was an imposing-looking man and not someone that Sean had met before.

"There's been a change of plan. Come with me." The man turned on his heel and walked away, leaving Sean sat, open-mouthed, and staring after him. He shook himself before standing up and following the man. Sean was feeling better after a night's rest, however he was still finding it difficult to keep up with the man.

"What's the change of plan?" Sean shouted. He had a right to know what was happening to himself and the lack of information was making him uneasy.

"I'll tell you once you're there." The man had stilled as he waited for Sean to catch-up. The man moved so quickly that Sean barely had time to register what was happening. Before he knew it, the man was securing handcuffs around his wrists. "Sorry, but I was told not to take any risks with you." The man pulled Sean along as he tried to make sense of what was happening.

Once they were outside, he was helped into the back of a prison van. The door shut, and the silence engulfed Sean. What had happened overnight for plans to change? Sean wanted to lash out and punch the inside of the van, however he knew from experience that it would only cause him more pain and wouldn't get him any answers. Instead, he focused on his breathing, trying to relax so that he could ask the right questions when the time came.

Sean soon found himself outside HM Prison Manchester. His escort had thrown open the doors to the van, and Sean stared open-mouthed at the menacing building. The man pulled at him to climb out of the van.

"What's going on?" Sean tried to pull back, but the man's grip on him was too strong.

"Your supervisor is inside and he'll explain. Don't draw too much attention to yourself." Sean did as he was told and dutifully followed the police officer into the prison and past the security. They took him straight to the isolation wing where his supervisor was waiting for him.

"Thank you, that will be all." Sean's escort was dismissed.

"What's happening?" Sean's wrists had been freed from the cuffs, however he had been ushered inside the cell and his supervisor had shut them in. There was no escaping.

"There's been further developments. The gang knew where you were being transported to and the house burned down. We need to keep you safe. Nobody here knows your true identity. We've created a false report for you, and you will stay in isolation for the time being. As soon as we can move you to a safe house, we will." Sean's supervisor looked worried, which told Sean how serious the situation was. Despite this, Sean was not concerned for his own safety. There was only one person he cared about.

"Is Laura safe?" A sob rose in Sean's chest. What if she had been in the house during the fire?

"She wasn't at the safe house when the fire began. We'll do our best to keep her safe. I have to go now. Sean, please behave. Your life depends on it."

The door closed and reality set in. He was in prison. These four walls would be all he knew for the foreseeable.

CHAPTER TWENTY TWO

Sean spent twenty-three hours in solitary confinement. The remaining hour was usually spent exercising on his own. For the first few weeks he had kept a record of the passing days, however he soon gave up. He suspected he had now been at Strangeways for almost six months. It was half a year since he had last held Laura, and yet she was all that he thought about. His cell was bare - the four walls painted in a depressing beige. There was just a small single bed and a desk furnishing the space. Sean spent every waking hour thinking, lost in his thoughts. Occasionally he would try reading, however his thoughts would soon steal away his attention. He would think about what Laura was doing. He only hoped that she had made it to another safe house and was not being kept imprisoned in solitary confinement like himself. As the weeks passed, Sean could feel himself slipping further and further away from reality. He was incandescent with rage. Six months in prison for trying to do his job. He had also had no contact with the outside world. Sean only hoped that no news was good news.

The first few weeks had been the worst. Sean had lashed out at a prison guard, which had resulted in his hour of exercise being stopped for two weeks. He hadn't tried that again. It was hard knowing that all of this was just to keep him safe.

Today, Sean was lying on his bed waiting for his lunch to be pushed through the hatch. The food was disgusting, but at least it broke the day up. It gave him something to focus on. There was a noise outside the door and Sean sat up, ready to collect his food once someone pushed it through. However, the door opened and a single man stood on the other side - he wasn't a prison guard.

"Mr Scott?" The man asked, checking that he had the right person. Sean nodded in response. "I'm here to drive you to the safe location." Sean blinked in shock. He wasn't aware of any plans to move him. It could be a trap but Sean didn't care, this was his chance to get out of this cell.

"Where are we going?" Sean questioned as he followed the man off of the isolation wing.

"I'm afraid I'm not permitted to tell you until we're on the road. We don't want anyone overhearing. Try not to draw any attention to yourself. The guards think you're being transferred to another prison." The man turned to him, his eyes pleading with him to understand. Sean understood that secrecy was imperative, and so he followed the man without protesting.

The car waiting out the front had blacked-out windows. Despite Sean's extensive knowledge of cars, he couldn't quite decipher what make it was. Someone had obviously customised it, and Sean suspected that the darkened windows would be made with bulletproof glass. He wondered whether Laura had received the same level of security, he could only hope that she had. The driver directed Sean to the backseat, informing him he would be safer there should anyone catch up with them.

Sean looked out of the window as the car sped off. They made their way out of Manchester and joined the motorway heading north. It was nice to be out in the open world again. He could finally re-unite with Laura.

"Can you tell me where we're going?" Sean asked again. He hated not being in control of the situation.

"Edinburgh." Silence echoed throughout the car as Sean let it sink in. He had never even been to Scotland before.

CHAPTER TWENTY THREE

Sean opened his eyes to see that it was dusk outside. In a matter of minutes, the last light would fade. He must have fallen asleep quite early into the journey, as he had very little recollection of the route they had taken. Despite the waning light, Sean recognised the gothic architecture of Edinburgh. Although he had never visited, he had seen the city on television and read about it enough times to know that this must be it. Under any other circumstances he would have been marvelling at his surroundings, taking it all in to tell Laura. The thought of Laura sent his mind spinning out of control. He hoped she had already taken this route, she'd already seen these buildings, and that she was waiting for him at the safe house.

"Are we far?" Sean asked, his voice was still gruff from sleep. He rubbed his eyes and tried to sit up straight in an attempt to wake himself up. He needed to be alert when they got out of the car, just in case somebody had followed them. Sean was hopeful that the gang would not be expecting him to depart from prison.

"Not far now, only about another ten minutes." The driver responded, keeping his eyes firmly on the road in front. Sean knew from experience that his driver was far more than just a chauffeur. He would be fully trained to protect Sean should anything go wrong. There would also be another car following them, filled with trained officers. Sean had been a part of this procedure enough times to know how well protected he was, he had just never expected to be the one in protective custody.

The driver had been correct in his estimation of ten minutes as nine and a half minutes later the car pulled to a stop outside a rather depressing looking house. Gone was the grand gothic architecture of Edinburgh city centre. They were now on the outskirts of the city, in the midst of a housing estate. Sean looked out onto a sea of grey houses with numerous blocks of flats towering over the estate. It was worlds away from the flat Sean shared with Laura, but for now it would do. For the time being they wouldn't be allowed outside the house, but that didn't matter. The only thing that mattered was that they would be together again after six long months.

Once all the checks had been done, an officer opened Sean's car door for him and led him to the front door. Two more officers were standing behind him. As the door swung open, Sean couldn't help but notice it was a composite door - one of the strongest on the market. They weren't taking any chances with their safety. With this in mind, Laura engulfed his thoughts and all he could think about was seeing her again. He was eager to wrap his arms around her and to hold her in his embrace. To know that she was safe and that he was there to protect her. Following the officers into the house, Sean looked around. It was bleak but liveable. The hallway walls were a grubby magnolia colour and not a single picture hung on them.

It almost reminded him of the properties that the organised crime group owned, each one devoid of anything personal.

Sean walked down the small hallway and into the living room, where two men were sitting waiting for him. Both were dressed in jeans and a plain top, however Sean could see the outline of a gun in their waistband.

"Mr Scott, this is Paul and Carl, both of whom are here for your protection." The police officer who led Sean into the house motioned for Sean to take a seat so that he could speak. With a sigh, Sean did as he was told. He already knew the protocol for protective custody, however he understood the officer would be obliged to talk him through it.

"Mr Scott, you will stay here for the foreseeable future. You're not allowed any contact with the outside world. Paul and Carl are here for your safety, but also to ensure that you stay within the confines of the property. There will also be plain clothed police officers patrolling outside. When possible, Paul and Carl will communicate any updates to you. Do you have any questions?" The officer finished his spiel and gave Sean a tight smile. He obviously just wanted to begin the long journey home.

"What's been happening for the past six months?" Sean's question was met with silence as the officers all looked at each other. "Okay, forget that question. Laura can fill me in. Where is she?" The excitement was bubbling inside of Sean. Despite the dingy house and being under house arrest, at least he would be with Laura and they could make the most of it. This would be the perfect opportunity to enjoy each other's company.

"Oh, hasn't anybody told you?" The man named Paul stood up, his tone filled with pity. A chill settled over Sean. What had happened to Laura?

"Where is she?" he asked. His hands were trembling and he could feel the room begin to spin around him. He had spent the last six months thinking she was safe. It was the only thing that kept him sane whilst staring at the same four walls.

"We're not sure." The man replied. His tone was completely devoid of any emotion, which only fuelled Sean's anger. How dare they leave Laura in such danger?

"What happened?" Sean growled through clenched teeth. His fists were balled up next to him as he tried to control the anger that was threatening to overcome him. Why wouldn't they tell him anything? How could they not know where she was? Sean did his best to channel his police training and to clear his mind before it could start conjuring up potential scenarios in which the gang captured Laura.

"There were officers stationed at the flat waiting for her to come home. The plan was to place her in immediate protective custody. We're not entirely sure what went wrong. She came home to the flat, that much we know, as she came across the bloody scene that you left behind. After that, a neighbour raised the alarm and tried to keep her calm whilst the police came. This neighbour has told us that Laura left with two officers. However, there's no official record of anyone escorting her to safety. We're unsure whether it was a rogue officer or just a gang member pretending. The plain clothed police officers that were stationed at the flat have said that they were relieved from their position by other officers. We suspect these people were also either rogue or fake." As the officer finished his explanation, Sean tried to take in the information that he had just been given. Whether they were fake officers or just rogue officers, it didn't matter, because either way Laura was in grave danger.

"So after all this, they've still captured Laura? And nobody thought to tell me during the last six months." Sean asked, his voice was shaking with emotion. A mixture of fear, anger and despair filled him - making it almost impossible to function.

"It's possible that she's escaped. We've been using CCTV to track the car she left in, and it looks as though she got away. We're combing more footage to locate her."

Sean couldn't speak, his heart was aching too much for the woman he loved. He was supposed to protect her, and yet he had put her in unimaginable danger. A red fog clouded his vision. He was angry at himself, angry at the gang, and he was angry at the officers who had failed to protect her. Sean was vaguely aware of the officers announcing that they would show him to his room. They escorted him upstairs. His legs were moving, but he didn't know how, his mind was too full to comprehend what was going on around him. Soon they reached the top of the stairs and he was gently pushed into the room by one of the officers.

"Get some rest." They instructed him before closing the door. The sound of bolts being slid across the door pulled Sean back to the present. He was stuck in Edinburgh under the watchful eyes of countless police officers. Meanwhile, Laura was alone and running for her life. There was nothing he could do to help her. Throwing himself onto the bed, Sean let out a scream of anguish before he was overcome with heart-wrenching sobs.

CHAPTER TWENTY FOUR

The days had all merged into one, but slowly the weeks were passing. Sean was being kept locked in his room at the safe house, out of fear that he might abscond if allowed to roam around the house. Every day he begged for an update as to Laura's whereabouts, and yet each day he was told they still didn't know where she was. Sean knew that this was bad news, there was no way Laura could evade police surveillance, something must have happened to her.

A knock on Sean's door made him jump. The officer named Paul came into his room with breakfast on a tray.

"Here you go," he said, placing the tray down on the bedside table. The room was sparse with only a single bed, a bedside table and a barren desk in the corner. It was depressing, but that was the least of Sean's worries. At least it was an upgrade from the prison cell they had kept him in. Occasionally, Sean would look out of the bedroom window, watching as spring slowly arrived.

"Any news?" Sean asked, it was more out of habit than anything. Whenever Paul or Carl entered the room, he would ask for an update and they always replied saying they didn't know anything.

"No, but I've requested a computer. I thought perhaps you might like to look through the CCTV footage yourself? After all, there's nobody better than you to spot Laura in a crowd. Also, I'm not sure how well they're looking for Laura. You're the main target, so all the resources seem to have been focused on you."

Sean could have leapt forward and hugged Paul. It was a brilliant idea; he didn't know why he hadn't thought of it himself. Sitting here doing nothing was soul destroying, but if he had the right equipment, at least he could do something to contribute towards getting Laura to safety. Paul was right, Laura was just another missing woman. There were too many missing people for them to focus too many resources on her.

By the beginning of June, they had transformed the downstairs dining room into a technology hub. In the middle of the room sat a gigantic desk with five big screens surrounding it, each playing footage from various CCTV sources. Because of the secrecy of Sean's location they, had not been able to have any IT people in to set the system up, and so it had taken the three men a frustrating amount of time to get the screens up and running. After four days, it was finally in action. Sean sat down, finally ready to flick through the different screens.

It had been eight months since Laura had gone missing. Sean was trying to ignore how impossible the task seemed. How would he ever find Laura amongst all those months of CCTV footage? With some trepidation, Sean began to watch the hours of footage. He located the CCTV surrounding the flat in hope that he could follow Laura's moves from the day she went missing. He watched in horror as Laura was escorted out of the building by two men he recognised. They were the same two men who had shot him.

"Is that her?" Paul asked. He was sitting next to Sean, watching the footage.

"That's her and they're the men that tried to kill me." Sean's face was ashen and his voice was little more than a whisper. With a newfound frenzy, he tracked Laura's movements through the CCTV. He watched as the car drove for a while. Eventually, it came to a halt at a cross-road. Despite the fuzzy picture from the traffic cameras, Sean could see the backdoor open and Laura sprung out and ran. The two men immediately sprinted after her, leaving the car abandoned at the lights. Sean's breath caught in his throat as he watched them chase her. They were mere feet from her. Was it possible that she had got away from them?

"Where does she go next?" Paul questioned, he was leaning closer to the screen and squinting as they both tried to track Laura's movements.

"I'm not sure." Sean was frustrated. Laura was ducking in and out of side streets, and soon there would be no CCTV for them to track the rest of her movements.

"Let's bring back the footage from the car and see what happened to it." Paul suggested and Sean pressed a few buttons so that the screen flickered back to the traffic camera. The car was abandoned at the lights, with the doors flung open. Cars were beeping it and angrily driving around it, however there was no driver in sight. Both men held their breath as they continued to watch the car to see whether the men returned to it. After what seemed like an eternity, they watched as the two men walked back up to the car and got in. Laura wasn't with them.

"She got away." Sean breathed a sigh of relief and his body relaxed into the chair he was sitting on. He hadn't realised just how tense he had been as he forced his jaw to unclench.

"I wonder where she went." Paul was thinking out loud with his comment so Sean didn't bother to reply - he was busy thinking the same.

Although he now knew that she had escaped, he had no leads on where to find her. He would have to comb through every inch of CCTV and that could take years.

CHAPTER TWENTY FIVE

Sean quickly fell into a routine. He was either sleeping or looking for Laura on the CCTV. Even during meal times he would eat at the desk watching the screens, not worrying about whether he dropped food down himself. He would only go to bed when his eyes stung so much that he knew his chances of missing her were high. Paul and Carl offered to go through footage whilst he slept but Sean declined, he was terrified they might miss something. Instead, they took turns sitting next to him and helping him comb through the footage. Sean suspected they were also staying close by in case he escaped. They had already taken a risk by letting him out of the bedroom. Both men seemed nice, they each had families at home and were eager for the operation to be over so they could return to their loved ones. Each day, Sean felt a sense of guilt that he was keeping them from their families, however he took comfort in the fact that at least they knew their families were safe.

With each day that passed, Sean grew more and more desperate to find Laura. He couldn't understand how she had avoided the police for so long. They had access to the same CCTV as Sean did, and yet neither of them had located her. It was the twenty fourth of June when Sean located her boarding a train at Manchester station. Glancing at the date, Sean realised Laura had got on this train only a day or two after she had fled from the gang. He was paralysed with fear as he realised that by now she could be anywhere in the world. If the police couldn't locate her in Manchester, how would they find her now?

"Anything?" Carl asked as he approached the desk. He could see by the look on Sean's face that something had happened.

"I've found her getting on a train, two days after she escaped the gang." The screen was frozen on her image. She had been dressed in black with a hoody pulled up to hide her face. If it hadn't been for a slight glance back as she boarded the train, he never would have known it was her.

"Let's find where the train was going." Carl suggested as he sat down next to Sean and tapped away at the screen. It only took them a few minutes to discover that Laura had boarded a direct train to London Euston.

"She's in London." Sean whispered, staring incredulously up at Laura's image. His sweet natured girlfriend had been forced to run all the way to London in search of safety.

"Unless, she's moved on." Carl was right, it was possible that Laura may have only gone to London to confuse anyone following her. Sean's thoughts had wandered back to the time he took her away to London as a surprise. Their time together had been magical.

"Should I phone this in and tell them?" Carl asked just as Paul entered the room to see what all the talking was about.

"Phone what in?" Paul asked, pulling up the spare seat.

"Sean's found Laura boarding a train to London." Carl explained, his hand hovering above his phone, waiting to dial the number.

"Hold on, let's talk this through for a moment." Paul said, moving Carl's phone, so it was out of reach. Sean was shocked by Paul's movement and turned to face him, waiting to see what he had to say for himself.

"We know that there are some rogue officers, right? If we feedback Laura's location, then we don't know who is going to be privy to that information." Paul's eyes were wide as he explained the logic behind his suggestion. Sean was stunned as he considered what Paul had said. It hadn't even crossed his mind that feeding back Laura's location could put her in more danger. He was so focused on finding her that nothing else had mattered.

"You're right. We can't tell anyone, we have to track her down ourselves." Sean agreed, running his hand through his hair. He was stressed and tired, but he would not give up for anything. He loved Laura with all of his heart, and he had to know she was okay. If she wasn't, then there was nothing left for him to fight for.

"Okay. We don't tell anyone. Somehow we need to get permission to view London CCTV. We know what train she was on and so we should be able to see her get off the train and track her movements from there." Carl was quick to piece together a plan for their next steps.

"I'm an undercover officer so it shouldn't take much for me to get permission to view the CCTV and it should be untraceable. My supervisor can approve it. It's the least he can do after leaving me locked up with no knowledge of the danger Laura has been in." Finally, Sean was seeing some perks to his undercover work.

After completing the forms, Sean had to wait to hear back and so for the first time in a long while he took a break. Carl grabbed a few bottles of beer from the fridge and the three men sat down in front of the television. As Sean watched the screen in front of him, he suddenly realised that it was Laura's birthday tomorrow. She always made a big point of how it was exactly six months from Christmas Day. As Sean sat sipping his beer, his mind wandered back to his last Christmas with Laura.

24th December 2018,

Christmas carols filled Sean's ears as he sat on the sofa watching Laura wrap the last-minute presents they had bought. It had been the usual frenzied trip into town when Laura remembered she had forgotten a present for someone. This year it had been her brother. They had walked hand in hand through the crowds of people to find the perfect present. Once the present had been found - an almost impossible to find PlayStation game - they treated themselves to hot chocolates and mince pies from one of their favourite independent cafes. As they sat and watched, the people pass them by, laden down with carrier bags, Sean couldn't help but dream of next Christmas. He had plans to make it their best Christmas yet.

"Could you grab me the other roll of tape?" Laura asked, pulling him from his daydreams. Sean smiled back at her and jumped up to go in search of the tape. His mind kept wander-

ing to the little envelope that was under the tree - his present to Laura.

Excitement filled him as he thought about her reaction when she opened the envelope. He was going to give it to her tonight, in private, rather than waiting for Christmas Day when they would be surrounded by family and friends.

Laura finished wrapping the presents and put them under the tree, where the lights were twinkling, casting a magical glow across the room.

"Hot chocolate?" She smiled up at Sean, already knowing his answer. Together, they made their way into the kitchen and made two gigantic hot chocolates covered in cream, marshmallows, a chocolate flake, and a dash of Irish Cream.

Once sat back in the living room, Sean watched as Laura took a sip from her drink, leaving behind a cream moustache. He laughed and took a picture of her before she could wipe it away.

"That's next year's Christmas cards sorted," he joked as he stared lovingly down at the picture. Laura rolled her eyes and tried not to laugh.

"I don't know how we're going to get all these presents round to my parents tomorrow." She sighed, staring at the mountain of gifts under the tree. They were having Christmas at the Harper's this year, and Sean's family would join them.

"I know, why don't I give you your present now? One less present to carry tomorrow." Sean's chest puffed out. He was rather proud of himself for smoothly suggesting she open her gift tonight.

"Are you sure?" she asked, he could see the excitement in her *eyes as she turned to look at the presents, wondering which one was hers. Sean couldn't help but laugh to himself. She was going to get a shock when she saw how small the present was.*

Sean walked over to the tree and picked up the envelope. It was gold, and he had simply written 'Laura' on the front. He saw the look of confusion cross her face briefly before she plastered on a fake look of excitement. Sean knew what she had been hoping for, she'd dragged him past enough jewellers over the past two months to have got the hint. However, he was playing the long game.

He handed her the envelope and watched as she undid it and read the piece of paper that he had carefully handwritten and placed inside. He had spent so long trying to find the perfect words that they were forever etched into his brain.

Dear Laura,

Merry Christmas. Or should I say Merry Christmas Eve?

I racked my brains about what to get you this year; I know over the years some presents have gone down better than others. I definitely misjudged the situation the year I bought you a new ironing board. I've learned my lesson and this year I wanted to get you something really special. This year I'm giving you next Christmas.

Christmas 2019 will be spent curled up in front of a roaring fire, sipping hot chocolate at an Austrian ski lodge. I have booked everything for our dream holiday and I cannot wait to spend it with you.

I love you,

Sean

A range of emotions flashed across Laura's face from excitement, happiness, to pure joy. A smile took over her face. She put the letter down and flung her arms around Sean's neck, thanking him over and over.

"Are you happy with your gift?" he asked her once she had finally let go of him and sat back down.

"Sean, it's perfect. I know we've talked about doing this for years, but just never got round to booking it. I can't wait."

Sean smiled to himself. He was proud of getting Christmas right this year. It also meant that he had a year to find the perfect ring and make next Christmas unbeatable.

"Do you want another beer?" Paul's gruff voice pulled Sean from his memories. He let out a long sigh and nodded to Paul. Christmas 2019 had been all planned out, however, instead of curling up in front of a roaring fire he had passed the day in a cold cell on his own. How a year could change your life.

CHAPTER
TWENTY SIX

Sean spent Laura's birthday sat in front of the television with Paul and Carl, watching rubbish films. Frustration filled Sean as he wiled away the hours, waiting for his authorisation to access the CCTV from London. That evening, Sean sat in front of the computer re-watching all the CCTV footage of Laura that he had found so far. He watched her run from the car. Despite knowing that she had escaped, he still felt her fear. All he wanted was to hold her in his arms again and to shelter her from the world. His job was to protect people and yet he couldn't protect those closest to him.

"Do you want another beer?" Paul asked, walking past Sean on his way to the kitchen.

"Yes, please." Sean replied before draining the dregs of the bottle in his hand. Tomorrow the drinking would stop so that his mind was coherent and he could concentrate on helping Laura. For now, he just had to get through each hour.

Paul handed Sean his beer and took the seat next to him. They both sat in silence for a few minutes, staring at the screen as they watched Laura run on repeat.

"Sean, I know your undercover operation was top secret, but what happened?" Paul's voice was timid, he knew it was a question that he shouldn't be asking. Sean thought for a moment. He shouldn't tell anyone what happened, however he had little left to lose and Paul had given up so much to protect him.

"I was given an undercover project. So secret that nobody at my station was aware of it. I knew it would be dangerous, but I enjoyed that aspect of my job and I know that if I can do my job well, then I'll be making a huge difference. The brief was to infiltrate one of the biggest drug operations in the north." Sean took a pause for breath as he remembered the day he walked into the office to accept the role. He had been full of enthusiasm and assured the head of the operation that he was the right man for the job.

"I was warned how dangerous it would be and told that nobody could know what I was up to. We don't know how many, but there are a lot of corrupt police officers in on the operation. I was also aware that I wasn't the only undercover officer. One of the existing undercover officers, Sam, introduced me to the gang and told them I wanted in. From there it was all about trying to gain their trust." Sean's voice broke off as he remembered back to the early days of joining the gang. The first two weeks he stayed at a hotel to protect Laura, in case they discovered his true identity. He didn't want anything leading back to her. In order to gain their trust, he had to do a lot of things he wasn't comfortable with. Sean had taken drugs, travelled with others to deliver drugs, and he had even sat back and watched as the gang plied young girls with drugs until they were comatose. It had been awful to have to stand in silence and watch as the events unfolded before him.

"What happened?" Paul questioned as he saw the dark look that crossed Sean's face.

"It was horrible." Sean sighed and tried to piece together the events in his head so that he could coherently retell the story. "Eventually, they accepted me into the gang, however, with acceptance came responsibility. I was running drugs for them, forced to take drugs, and worst of all I was encouraged to sell drugs to vulnerable people. I'll never forgive myself for that, I overstepped the mark, but I was so intent on being accepted into their group."

"What went wrong?" Paul could tell Sean was finding it difficult to retell the story, and so he tried to encourage him to move on to the most important part.

"I stole cocaine from them." The room was filled with a tense silence as the words sunk in.

"You stole drugs from the most dangerous gang in the north?" Paul asked. His eyes were wide with terror.

"There's more to it. I was given drugs to sell. There was a bad batch and people were dying. I had to take a sample so that we could link the gang to the deaths. However, once I was in the warehouse and faced with the cocaine, I couldn't just walk away. I took it all. How could I leave it there and allow others to die?" Sean took a long swig of his beer as he waited for Paul to digest what he had just told him. "After they lost the drugs, they suspected many of us were responsible. Steps were taken to protect my identity. I lost my job at my station and was wiped from the system in case any of the corrupt officers tried to find information on me. The police did everything they could to protect my true identity, however it wasn't enough. A few weeks later they discovered who I was. Another undercover officer revealed my identity. Those two that kidnapped Laura were the ones that came to the flat. I had a rare morning off and was planning on meeting a few members of the gang for a beer that evening and so when the doorbell went I didn't think much of it. I went to answer it, but there was no answer. The next thing I knew someone had picked the lock to my front door and two men were standing in my living room with guns." Sean was overcome by emotion as he recalled those terrible events as the men stood in his flat, accusing him of being an undercover officer. He had tried to deny it, but he knew that it was too late. When they shot him, he knew his only chance was to run, otherwise he would end up dead.

"You've been through a lot." Paul commented as he let out a long breath. His face gave away the fear that he was now feeling after hearing Sean's story.

"It's still not over." Sean sighed, downing the rest of his beer in an attempt to numb the emotions that he had just stirred up.

The two of them sat in silence until Paul excused himself and went to bed. Meanwhile, Sean stared at the screen in front of him. He had it paused on a frame of Laura where he could almost see her face. He longed to see her again, to hold her, to watch her eyes sparkle as he teased her, but most of all he just wanted to know that she was okay.

CHAPTER TWENTY SEVEN

A few days later, Sean got the good news that he had been waiting for, he could access the London CCTV. With a large cup of coffee in his hand, he began by locating the footage from the day Laura travelled to London. He watched as she climbed off the train at London Euston. Her eyes were darting in all directions and she was quick on her feet. Sean could only imagine what was going through her head in that moment. Over the next few days, Sean continued to frantically capture glimpses of Laura on the grainy CCTV. It was torture watching her dart from one area to another; she was searching for safety. Some nights, Sean had begged Paul and Carl to turn a blind eye so he could escape, however they refused and reminded him that even if he tried, the plain clothed officers outside would stop him. He was trapped and all he could do was sit back and watch as Laura struggled through each day.

Sean tried to skip through as much footage as possible - searching for clues as to where she was. He eventually found her again, sleeping on the streets. She begged for food and slept in doorways. Sean was on the verge of losing his sanity as his heart broke each day. The only thing that kept him going was that he was sure one day they would be together again and life would return to some form of normality. Summer passed in a blur and Paul and Carl were relieved by two other officers, neither of whom spoke to Sean. That was okay though, Sean didn't much feel like talking to them, all he ever wanted to do was watch Laura.

From what Sean could see, her behaviour was becoming increasingly erratic, and Sean was becoming progressively worried about her. One particularly dreary morning, he was sitting watching her, coffee in hand. She looked distracted as she walked against the flow of morning commuters. Her face was withdrawn and despite not being able to see her eyes, he knew they no longer held that mischievous sparkle that he loved so dearly. It happened in slow motion, Sean brought his cup of coffee up to his mouth just as Laura stepped out into the road.

"No!" he screamed. It was a natural reaction, although he knew she wouldn't be able to hear him. The bus hit and Sean watched as Laura's body crumpled under the weight of the impact. By now, he had spilt his coffee down himself and the boiling liquid was seeping through his jogging bottoms. However, it was the least of his worries. His eyes didn't leave the screen in front as he lost control of his emotions. His body slumped in the chair and heart-wrenching sobs tore through his body. People crowded around Laura's lifeless body and Sean held his breath as he waited for an ambulance to arrive. It looked as though there was someone performing first aid on her. The picture was too grainy to see exactly what was happening, but eventually they had Laura on a stretcher and they put her into the back of the ambulance.

What now? Sean thought to himself. This had happened almost a month ago. How would he know she was okay? Without thinking it through, Sean knew he had to escape this house. He had to look for Laura. Sean knew it would be difficult, but he had to; he couldn't just leave Laura hurt and in danger. What if something terrible had happened to her? That footage had been a month old. Anything could have happened to her since. Blinded by emotions, Sean told the two officers that he was just popping out to the garden for some fresh air. They grunted in response and turned their attention back to the television. Sean let out a sigh of relief. At least they wouldn't notice his absence. For months now he had been forming an escape plan in his head. The garden had an alleyway that ran along the back of it, and despite the plain clothed officer's best attempts, there were not enough of them to be on patrol all the time.

Silently, Sean tiptoed to the back of the garden, to where the fence was slightly lower, he peeped over to check that none of the officers were currently patrolling. It was clear. Sean said a silent prayer for all of his years of police training that allowed him to bolt, nimbly, over the fence. As his feet hit the ground in the alleyway, he had to make a snap decision whether to go left or right. He chose right. He stealthily made his way to the end of the alleyway and checked to see whether anyone was around. There was an elderly man across the road walking his dog, however, Sean reasoned with himself - it was unlikely that an undercover officer would be that old or have a dog with them. Taking the chance, Sean jogged down the road, thankful that he was wearing jogging bottoms and so could easily pass for someone out for their morning exercise.

Before he got even halfway down the street, someone reached out and grabbed his shoulder, making him stop. Sean slowly turned to face the person. He didn't know whether it would be a member of the gang or an officer standing behind him. He wasn't sure which one he dreaded the most. A sense of relief rushed over Sean as he realised it was a plain clothed officer. He recognised the man who would often walk past the house multiple times a day.

"Where are you going?" The man's voice had somewhat of a threatening edge to it.

"Please, just let me go. Pretend you haven't seen me." Sean begged, it was his only chance. He had got this far, he couldn't go back now.

"I'm afraid I can't. Come on, let's go back." The man was surprisingly strong as he ushered Sean back down the road and through the front door to his prison.

"You're not keeping a very good watch!" The officer chastised the two men that were supposed to be babysitting Sean.

"Sean, you know you're not supposed to go anywhere." The nicer of the two men stood and gestured for Sean to take a seat.

"Laura's been run over." Sean couldn't risk keeping her location a secret anymore. He had to hope for the best.

"You know where Laura is?" The other officer asked. Sean took a deep breath to stop the sob from escaping his body before he sat up straight and told the officers the date and the location of where Laura had been hit by the bus. They promised him they would find out whatever they could. Sean knew the dangers in sharing her location, however, as it had happened a month ago, he hoped she had already recovered and gone somewhere safe. He had to know that she was okay.

They left Sean sitting in the living room with the officer that had found him on the street. They turned on the television and both stared blindly at it as the other officers made calls in the kitchen. Somehow, Sean sat there and waited for news. He didn't know how he achieved it, but he was on his best behaviour. His mind was miles away, wondering how Laura was, whether she was in pain or even alive. Sean felt sick as the memory of the bus hitting her replayed over and over in his mind. He hated that he hadn't been there to protect her. What if she'd died last month and didn't know?

"She's alive." One of the officers announced as he walked back into the room. He took a seat opposite, before explaining the news to Sean. "We believe she's going under the name of Claire, she's the only person that fits Laura's description that was involved in a road traffic accident on that date."

"How certain are you that it's her?" Sean asked, he couldn't allow himself to get his hopes up if it was possible that it wasn't her.

"Almost certain. There are no other women around her age, with her description, that was involved in an accident in London on that date." The officer looked frustrated as he repeated what he had just told Sean.

"Okay, and is she safe?"

"We have no reason to believe that she isn't. I've tried to be discreet in asking for information. Do you want the police to search the hospital footage and try to track her from there?"

Sean thought about it for a minute. He had to make the right decision; it was his only opportunity to protect Laura.

"Okay. Let them track her. What hospital was she taken to? I want to track her, too" Sean was finding it difficult to stay still. He was eager to discover where Laura had been taken to and to start watching the CCTV.

"Guy's Hospital." As soon as the words were out of the officer's mouth, Sean leapt up and went to locate the CCTV. He would go through the CCTV to find the footage of Laura leaving the hospital to make sure she was okay.

CHAPTER TWENTY EIGHT

Twenty-four hours passed, and Sean still hadn't found Laura leaving the hospital. He had been combing through the footage, trying to fast forward it now and then to speed up the process. However, he was afraid of missing Laura. There hadn't been any updates from the London police team. Sean had not slept yet. He'd lost count of how many cups of coffee he had drunk, and eventually he had to admit defeat and go to bed.

"Sean?" Somebody was shaking Sean awake. He tried to fight the consciousness, but it was no good.

"What's happening?" he asked as he tried to gain his bearings. All too soon everything came flooding back to him and he jumped up as one of the officers stood in his room looking concerned.

"The police in London have contacted us. They've told us what date Laura was discharged. Apparently a doctor discharged her, against the general advice of the hospital. They can't find her leaving the premises."

Sean pushed past the officer and ran downstairs to his computer. He sat impatiently tapping away at the keys as the machine switched on. The other officer entered the room and silently handed Sean a cup of coffee. He downed the coffee and waited for the caffeine to enter his system.

The three men watched the screens, waiting to see Laura emerge from the hospital. She was discharged earlier in the day, however it wasn't until the nighttime that Sean watched her leave the hospital and get into a taxi with a handsome young doctor. Jealousy coursed through his veins as he watched her with this man. Had she really given up on him so easily? He tried to put the jealousy aside and concentrate on following the taxi through the various CCTV cameras. Eventually, the car pulled up outside some flats and the two of them climbed out of the taxi and went inside the building. Sean couldn't bear to think what might have happened behind closed doors. Despite everything that he had gone through, his love for Laura had been what had pushed him to keep going. He loved her with all of his heart, and he had wanted to do everything possible to save her. Yet here she was, ready to move on with the first man she met. Perhaps she had spent the last month with the doctor whilst he sat frantically combing through all the footage.

Angrily, Sean shut down the computer, ignoring both of the men sitting either side of him, and stalked back up to his bedroom. If Laura didn't value their relationship enough to fight for him, then why should he waste his time thinking about her? He tossed and turned for a while, but eventually sleep won and he drifted off into a fitful slumber.

2nd September 2019,

Sean stared down at the bag of cocaine in his hands. It was yet another parcel ready for him to deliver to a customer. This was the part of the undercover work that Sean hated the most, he was at the frontline, encouraging others to ruin their lives and give their money to these criminals. Today was different though, today Sean was being given an apprentice. He was told that his apprentice was the son of the man at the centre of the operation and he was being sent out to see all aspects of the business. Sean was nervous. It seemed a bit odd for them to give him the apprentice, but he hadn't asked too many questions. That alone could have given him away.

Sean was sitting in one of the cars that had been loaned to him by the gang. They were known as 'pool' cars and the gang members would share them whilst they undertook gang work - otherwise known as criminal activity. The cars were stolen and false numbers plates were put on them to throw the police off.

A knock on the passenger window made Sean jump. A man climbed in and turned to face Sean.

"Nice to meet you, I'm Luke." He smiled over at Sean and reached his hand out to shake. Sean was taken back, this was not the man he had been expecting to take out as his apprentice. The man was good looking, well spoken, and above all he was wearing doctor's scrubs.

"Sorry, I was in a rush to get out of work, do you mind if we stop off somewhere so I can get changed?" Luke had noticed Sean's quizzical look towards his outfit.

"That's fine, we better get going or we'll be late."

Sean could remember that day as clear as anything, as it had been so odd. He chatted to Luke as they did their drops and they got on well. Usually, when Sean was in the car with other members of the gang, he was internally cringing the entire time as they dropped derogatory comments about women and told stories of various violent fights that they had been involved in. However, Luke told Sean about the patients he had been treating and Sean couldn't help but notice the emotion behind Luke's stories. He found it hard to believe that Luke could be the son of such a ruthless and violent man. When he voiced this out loud, Luke explained that nobody would suspect a doctor. He had a point.

Their time together had been short, but when Sean dropped the car back off and said goodbye to Luke, he had meant it when he said he hoped he saw him again.

With a jerk, Sean woke from the dream that he had been having. He didn't know what time of the day it was, but from the change in lighting in his room he guessed he had been asleep for quite a while. As he yawned and stretched, the dream came back to him, however it was not a dream, it had been a memory. Not only that, he now knew why the doctor that Laura had gone home with looked so familiar. It had been Luke. A mixture of emotions merged in Sean's head, making him temporarily paralysed. He didn't know what to do next. Luke must have charmed Laura somehow. Perhaps he had even suggested he knew where Sean was. Whatever had happened, Sean now knew for sure that Laura wouldn't have gone with Luke on her own accord and she was in danger.

Sean changed into a fresh pair of black jogging bottoms and grabbed a hoodie. In the corner of his room, a black bag had been discarded. It had been lying there for months, ever since Paul had dropped off some new clothes for him. Grabbing the bag, Sean stuffed some spare clothes into it and grabbed the bread knife that he kept under his pillow. Whatever happened, he had to save Laura. Nobody would stop him escaping this time.

CHAPTER TWENTY NINE

Laura Harper

12th January 2021

"The cast can come off now." The doctor smiled up at her as he glanced down at her x-ray one last time. Laura could barely believe what she was hearing. After weeks of having this stupid cast on her foot, she would now be free. She laid back on the doctor's examination bed and waited for him to gather the correct tools to remove the cast.

Silently, she watched as the doctor began the task. She was excited and relieved at the idea of soon being able to walk properly. That also meant she could soon run again. Meanwhile, the man that had accompanied her sat in the chair opposite the doctor's desk, quietly taking in the room around him. His name was Greg, and Laura owed her life to him.

As Laura laid on the bed, allowing the doctor to cut through the cast, her mind wandered back to her last day in the warehouse and the day she met Greg.

December 2020,

Time stilled as Laura realised she was about to die. Her eyes caught Luke's, and she saw they were filled with fear. Before Laura could say or do anything, a huge weight crashed into her, knocking her sideways and out of the way of the bullet. Someone was lying on top of her, shielding her from the violence. Laura tried to look up, but she regretted it immediately. She saw the moment a bullet hit Luke, his eyes went wide and blank, and he fell to the floor. Laura had to stop herself from screaming out. He was the whole reason she was there, she couldn't waste time feeling upset about him.

It seemed like Laura was on the ground for hours, the weight of the man on top of her was making it difficult to breathe.

"Stay calm, it's almost over." The man whispered in her ear as he tried to reposition himself so that his weight wasn't on her, but so he was still shielding her body. The man was dressed in the gang's uniform, which only confused Laura more. Thoughts were whirling around Laura's head as she tried to figure out what was going on. Why had this man saved her and stood by whilst Luke was killed? It made little sense.

Gun shots fired around her and the fear almost consumed Laura. She didn't know how she would ever make it out of here alive. As an image of Sean entered her mind, she wondered what he was doing right now. Had he come to save her? Hope filled her. She grabbed onto it and refused to let it go. She would get out of this alive and she would be reunited with Sean. He had come to save her.

Laura tightly closed her eyes, trying to ignore what was going on around her. The mystery man shielded Laura from the fight above them. She tried not to think about what was going on around her. However, the loud thump that echoed throughout the room every time a body fell to the ground was a stark reminder. She was in danger.

"Safe!" Someone shouted from above and Laura felt the weight of the man disappear. Before she could ask any questions, he picked her up from the ground and began to walk, whilst still carrying her.

"What are you doing?" she gasped out as her eyes surveyed the surrounding room. There were people lying on the ground, either dead or dying.

"Laura, we have to get you out of here and then we can discuss what's going on." His voice was reassuring and Laura gave up trying to fight. She didn't know who to trust anymore. She watched in disbelief as he peeled off his facial hair. The men surrounding her did the same. They had all been in disguise, completely blending in with the other gang members.

"Greg?" The weak voice of Luke called out. Laura turned to see Luke lying on the ground. His face was ashen and there was blood pooling around his torso. He was staring at the man who was holding onto Laura.

"You made your choice. Mum would be heartbroken." The mystery man carrying Laura spat back.

"Don't say that." Luke was visibly growing weaker, and his face was contorted in pain. Greg ignored his reply and walked out of the warehouse with Laura still in his arms.

Once they were outside, he set Laura down on her feet next to a plain white mini van. Laura blinked a few times, trying to adjust to the lighting. She didn't know how long she'd been trapped inside for. She didn't even know what the date was, she only hoped it was still December.

"What's going on?" Laura asked. She found that shielding her eyes helped her to see. Beside the mini van, were five men, three of whom were in the gang's uniform, whilst the other two were wearing jeans and a bullet-proof vest. Were they part of the gang? Part of another gang? Or perhaps they were with Sean?

"Get in the van and we'll tell you everything." One of the men opened the van door and gestured for her to get inside. Laura was reluctant to go anywhere with these men. What if she got herself into even more danger?

"Laura, my name's Greg. I promise you, we're here to help you. We have to be quick in case they called for help. More gang members might be on their way." Greg was the man who had been protecting Laura from the gunshots. With a sigh, Laura climbed into the van. It was her only option right now. This man had just saved her from the gang, and so she hoped she was right in putting her trust in him. She didn't want to make the same mistake twice.

As soon as everyone was in and the door was shut, the van sped off. Greg sat next to Laura and she turned to face him. She couldn't wipe the memory of Luke on the floor of the warehouse, slowing bleeding to death.

"What's going on?" she asked, whilst trying to brace herself against the side of the van as it swung around bends.

"We've been working undercover, just like Sean, although he didn't know about us. I'm sorry we couldn't get you away from Luke sooner, but we had to wait for the right moment." Greg paused for a moment to allow Laura to consider what he

had just said. All these men sat around her were undercover officers. But if Sean didn't know about them, then how could he be behind this?

"Where's Sean?" Laura asked, her voice was shaking as she realised he hadn't saved her. She had been longing to see him and to run into his arms.

"The last we heard was that he had been taken into protective custody and was being kept safe in a house up in Scotland."

Sean was in Scotland. Laura tried to calm her breathing as she processed all the information. Sean was okay, and she was going to be okay too. Everything was going to be okay.

"So are we going to Scotland now?" Laura's mind was wandering off with thoughts of her reunion with Sean.

"No, we're going into hiding. We thought Wales would be an excellent choice."

Laura was speechless. They were going into hiding.

Greg saw the look on her face and reached out to put a reassuring hand on her shoulder.

"It won't be for long, Laura, I promise. We're all in great danger at the moment, and I'm sure the top gang members will be after us. The majority of people in that warehouse were dressed in uniform, meaning they were at the bottom of the gang's hierarchy. There will be members who are higher up the chain looking for us. Until they're dealt with, we have to stay safe." Greg gave Laura's shoulder a reassuring squeeze.

"Luke knew you." Laura had too many questions to allow the conversation to end.

"We have history." Greg turned to look out of the window, in-

dicating that he no longer wanted to speak. Laura knew better than to keep pushing him.

That was it. Conversation over. Laura had so many questions buzzing around inside her head that she didn't even know where to start. She was away from the gang. Sean was safe, and she was about to go into hiding in Wales. Where, or how, did she even begin to process all of that information?

◆ ◆ ◆

"Can you point your toes forward, please?" The doctor pulled Laura from her memories with his question. He had taken the cast off of her foot. With a nod, Laura pointed her toes. She tried to focus on what she was doing, however her mind was still lingering on that day. She couldn't forget Luke's last glance. His eyes were filled with despair as he watched them leave. They had driven to Wales and rented a big house in the middle of nowhere for all six of them.

Every day waking up was awful. She was still separated from Sean. She feared for his safety. After everything that had happened, the gang wouldn't think twice about killing him. The days didn't get any easier as Laura forced herself to go through the motions of eating, washing and sitting in front of a television, blindly staring at its screen. She was slowly going mad, trapped inside the house. Occasionally, she had thought about trying to escape, but with five police men watching her it would be impossible.

"How does that feel?" The doctor asked as she stood up and attempted to walk. It was strange, the muscles were weak, and the absence of a heavy cast was bizarre. Yet at the same time she was ecstatic to have the use of her foot back.

They spent a few minutes doing some exercises and Laura was given a sheet with more exercises to continue at home. Once the appointment was over, she thanked the doctor and left the room with Greg close behind her. She never went anywhere without a bodyguard these days, you never knew who was lurking around a corner.

CHAPTER THIRTY

Once back at the house, Greg and Laura went their separate ways; Greg to play video games, while Laura went to make herself a coffee. She had never liked coffee much until Sean had introduced her to it. She still remembered that day as clear as anything.

5th January 2015,

"Come on Laura, this is boring." Sean whinged as he scuffed his feet on the floor. He was in a terrible mood, having been dragged around the January sales for hours.

"Look, Sean, half price!" Laura pointed excitedly at the mixer that was standing on display, a huge sale sign above it. Sean sighed as Laura tiptoed towards the object, almost scared that it would run away from her. Sean loved Laura, but sometimes her enthusiasm for kitchen gadgets was a little overwhelming. Perhaps that was just life with a budding chef.

"I'll make you a deal. You can buy the mixer if we can stop for a coffee after this." Sean held on to Laura's hands to get her attention as he spoke. Her eyes widened as she realised she could buy the mixer.

"Thank you! I'll bake you a cake tonight with it." She beamed back at him and chose the colour she wanted. Sean breathed

a sigh of relief as they stood at the checkout. He could see a coffee shop in the distance.

A few minutes later, they chose a table and put down all of their bags.

"You stay here with the bags and I'll order. What do you want?" Sean asked. He was finding it difficult to stay still with the promise of coffee only a few short steps away.

"Surprise me." Laura replied, somewhat absent-mindedly as she stared at the box holding her brand new mixer.

Sean made his way up to the counter and glanced at the menu board as he queued. For years he had been trying to get Laura to try coffee, but each time she refused. He knew that if she would only try it, she would love it. Sometimes, he knew her better than she knew herself. Sean bought her a coffee - a caramel cappuccino to be exact - if she didn't like it then he would just queue up again and buy her a hot chocolate.

"Thank you!" Laura smiled as he sat back down at the table. She had finally torn her eyes away from her new purchases. "I'm sorry for dragging you around the shops for hours looking at kitchenware."

Sean smiled at the guilty look that had crossed her face.

"It's okay, I know how much you enjoy your kitchen gadgets. At least I get to enjoy the food that you make with them."

They sat in silence for a few minutes, both enjoying the rest after hours of trailing round shops with the usual January sales crowds. Despite the chaos, and the endless shopping bags, it had been a lovely day. After having spent so long with family members over Christmas, it was nice just to be the two of them again.

Laura picked up her cup and brought it to her mouth. Her nose wrinkled as the smell of sweet coffee hit her senses. She narrowed her eyes at Sean, but she didn't back down from the challenge. Sean watched her face as she took her first sip. Her eyes relaxed as the coffee hit her taste buds.

"What do you think?" he asked. A smug feeling rising within him.

"It's really nice," she begrudgingly admitted. At least now, Laura could incorporate coffee into her recipes since she knew what it tasted like.

"I told you so." Sean beamed back at her, laughing slightly as he took a sip of his own drink. He was also somewhat relieved to know he wouldn't have to get up again and order her something different.

"Yeah, yeah. You know best, don't you?" Laura rolled her eyes but couldn't stop the smile that spread across her face.

The kettle boiled, forcing Laura to abandon her memories and return to the task at hand. She made her coffee and then went over to sit at the kitchen table. Her leg shook slightly as she put her weight down on her foot. It would take a while for walking to feel normal again. Laura had been amazed that her ankle had healed. After all that she had put it through, she had been dreading having to have it operated on.

"How did your appointment go?" A tall man with reddish hair sat down opposite her. His name was Jake, and he was one of her bodyguards. Well, technically, he was an undercover police officer, but Laura liked to think of them all as her bodyguards - it made her feel safer.

"My ankle is fixed." She smiled back at him. Some of her bodyguards were quiet and reserved, whereas Jake would often sit with her and talk.

"That's brilliant news!" Jake smiled back at her. Laura took a sip of her coffee and watched Jake over the top of her mug. His smile seemed strained, and he looked as though he had something he wanted to say to her.

"What's going on, Jake?" she asked, although she doubted she wanted to know the answer to her question.

"It's Sean. He's missing."

Those two words rattled around Laura's head as she allowed them to sink in. She had been happily living in the house for a while now. Being apart from Sean was difficult, not knowing whether he was safe. Having the confirmation that he was in danger only made things worse. Laura sat trembling as her mind considered the danger Sean could be in.

"What happened?" Laura took a deep breath to steady her voice. She had to find out what was going on before she allowed her emotions to take over.

"He has been watching CCTV of you in London and he saw you get hit by the bus. Apparently, he left shortly after. The officers tried to stop him but he threatened them with a knife."

Laura thanked Jake for telling her and then made her way up to her bedroom, slamming the door behind her. It was her fault that Sean had left the protection of his safe house. She wanted to feel his arms wrap around her and to reach up on her tiptoes to kiss him and tell him everything would be okay. They'd been apart for far too long. Laura knew she had to find him, but first she would need to get away from her bodyguards.

CHAPTER THIRTY ONE

Laura laid on her bed, moving her foot in circles. She was already starting on her exercises, knowing that she would need every bit of strength she could muster. Somehow, she had to get away from this house and her bodyguards. She had to find Sean. The only problem was, she didn't know how to do either. Walking out the door was hardly an option, and she did not know where in the world Sean was. Despite all this, Laura knew that sitting in this house waiting to be saved was not an option. She wanted her life with Sean back and to do that she had to get it back. This had gone on for far too long. It was time something changed and nobody seemed to be doing anything about it, and so it was time for Laura to act.

She sat up and commanded her brain to think. There had to be a way to get out of this mess. Laura wondered whether any of her bodyguards would help her. The only problem was, she could not risk asking them in case they said no. Her mind was whirling and her fists were balled up in anger. How had her almost-perfect life been so cruelly turned upside down? A knock on her bedroom door forced Laura to take a deep breath to calm down.

"Come in!" she called, trying to arrange her face into a

false smile. The last thing she wanted was to speak to someone.

Greg entered the room, a sombre look on his face. Without saying anything, he sat down on the bed next to her, putting an arm around her shoulders. Greg was the kindest out of her bodyguards. He always made sure she was okay and took the time to listen to her woes.

"I'm sorry, I've just heard the news about Sean." His voice was calm but Laura suspected he was hiding some emotion behind it.

"Greg, hypothetically, if I was considering something stupid, what would you say?" If anyone would support her in her quest to find Sean, it would be Greg.

"I'd say, when are we leaving?" Greg's reply took Laura by surprise. She hadn't expected him to be so encouraging. However, her mind flitted back to the warehouse when Luke had addressed him. Greg had unfinished business with the gang. Laura had questioned Greg about it, but he had not wanted to talk to her.

"Really?" Laura asked to check he wasn't teasing her.

"Laura, you're not the only one with a family back home. As much fun as this has been, I would like to get home to my husband before he turns grey. Also, I have my own score to settle with Harry." Greg had briefly spoken to Laura about the gang, he had been cagey but he had told Laura that he had some sort of history with the gang leader, Harry.

"Will you help me?" Laura held her breath as she waited for Greg to respond. Talking hypothetically was one thing, but asking an officer to go against his instructions and walk into the face of danger was a whole other thing. Time seemed to stand still as Greg considered her question. Would he agree to help her or would he put her under house arrest?

"I'll help you." His answer was short, but to the point.

"Okay. We need a plan."

They both sat there in silence for a few minutes as they tried to conjure up a plan. Laura couldn't envision any plan that would be successful. How on earth were they going to find Sean and protect themselves from an angry organised crime group?

"Should we involve anyone else?" Laura had been wondering whether to ask any of the other men to help them, but she wasn't sure.

"I don't think they'd be happy about it, Laura, and they might try to stop us from going." Greg presented a good argument, they had to be careful who knew their plan. It would just be the two of them.

"Okay, that's one aspect of the plan sorted. It's just the two of us. Where do we go?" It was one thing sneaking out of the house without being caught, but then where would they go? There was no point blindly driving around the country trying to hunt people down.

"I've got some contacts. I'll contact them and see whether they have any information." There was something about the way Greg spoke that reminded Laura of Luke. However, she shook her head and forced herself to cast the thoughts aside. Greg was nothing like Luke.

Laura was worried that she was being stupid by placing her trust in someone else. However, it was that or sit around waiting for someone else to make the first move.

"Tomorrow is our best chance of escaping. Jake and Sam are going food shopping so there'll be less of us. The others will probably just be playing games, so if we can get ourselves ready tonight, we'll leave tomorrow." It sounded silly, undercover officers going out to the supermarket, but it was a necessity - they couldn't risk having any online activity linking them back to this location. Today, however, Laura was very grateful that they had to go food shopping. At least it would be fewer officers to deceive.

"What do we need?" Laura asked, mentally making a list.

"Pack yourself a bag of clothes, maybe see if you can get some food from the kitchen. Can you shoot?" Greg's question caught Laura by surprise, but it was a valid point. They would need to protect themselves.

"I can, Sean taught me."

"I'll sort us some weapons, but you have to promise me you'll only use it if you absolutely have to. I could get in a lot of trouble for this."

"Are you sure about this, Greg? I'm happy to go on my own. All I ask is that you don't tell the others until I've got a head start." Laura meant what she said, she didn't want to drag other people into this mess.

"No, I want to help you. How could I sleep at night knowing I let you go on your own? I want to help you, and I want to help stop this gang. The sooner we do it, the sooner I can be back home with my family. Besides, I have a history with Harry and I'd like to see his face when he realises his time is up."

They finalised their plans, and both went their separate ways. Laura set about packing her bag. She had accumulated several toiletries and clothes from the officers' trips to the supermarket. Laura chose two outfits and folded them as small as possible into her bag. Once done, she tiptoed downstairs to steal some food from the cupboards. She would have to be careful not to raise any suspicions.

CHAPTER THIRTY TWO

The following morning, Laura watched from her bedroom window as Jake and Sam left in the white mini van to do the food shop. Her bag was packed, and she had just finished doing her daily foot exercises. Laura suspected there was going to be a lot of walking, and so she needed her foot to co-operate. A soft knock on the door made Laura jump. It was time. With a quick glance around the room, she grabbed her bag and headed to the door. Despite everything, she would miss this house. She had grown strangely attached to it. It was the first place she had been truly safe in over a year.

"You ready?" Greg whispered, careful not to draw attention to their conversation. The others were downstairs in the backroom playing video games.

"What's the plan?" Laura asked as she began her descent down the stairs, careful not to step on the one third from the bottom that squeaked.

"We're taking the other car. That way, even if they realise we've gone, they won't be able to catch us until the others are home from shopping." It was a good plan. Shortly after arriving in Wales they had realised they would need a second car and so the police arranged for a car to be delivered to them. Now all they had to do was to get outside and into the car, without anyone noticing. As Laura stepped onto the last step, her ankle give way and she fell. Quickly, she put her hand across her mouth to muffle her cries of pain.

"Laura, are you okay?" Greg asked her as he helped her back up. They both stilled, waiting to see whether anyone had heard. Would someone come and see what the noise was? They waited a couple of minutes, but nobody came.

"I'm fine. Just adjusting to using both legs again." The pain was slowly easing, and she could put some weight on her ankle. "Let's go."

Together, they made their way over to the door, opening it as quietly as possible, and slipping outside to where the car was waiting. Greg took Laura's bag from her and threw both bags in the backseat before he climbed into the front. It took Laura a little longer to get into the car, but once she was in they both shut their doors at the same time, Greg started the car and was out of the driveway before Laura could even put her seatbelt on. He had wanted to get away quickly in case the sound of the doors shutting drew any attention to them.

They both held their breath as they drove away from the house, checking the mirrors to see whether anyone had followed them. There was nobody around.

Laura took a few minutes to relax. Her foot was still throbbing, but hopefully the pain would ease as they drove. Speaking of driving, she didn't know where they were going.

"Did you hear back from your contacts?" she asked, hoping that someone might have been able to give Greg some information on where Sean was.

"He was spotted in Manchester, back at your flat. They sent officers to the address, but by the time they had arrived he had left. Their guess is that he had gone back for clothes. Apparently, the flat has been trashed, most likely by the gang. I think they went there after we escaped the warehouse. We're going to head to Manchester and see whether we can pick up a trail." Laura sighed, her beautiful flat had been trashed, again. She still remembered the day they had moved in.

10th November 2018,

"Miss, where do you want this?" One of the removal men asked, signalling towards the large box that he was carrying.

"I think it's for the kitchen." Laura replied, trying to keep her calm. 'Kitchen' was written in very large and eligible writing down the side and the top of the box.

"I know, miss. The problem is there are so many boxes in the kitchen we can't fit anymore in." Sean sniggered from behind the removal man, before quickly going to grab another box before Laura could throw something at him.

"Could you just start making a pile against the back wall in the living room?" Laura was beginning to wonder whether she had gone a little overboard with all of her kitchen purchases over the years. She had always justified them as 'work tools', however, in reality, she probably had a little bit of an addic-

tion to buying kitchen gadgets.

Once all the boxes were in and the removal men had left, Sean and Laura walked hand in hand to their local chip shop, ready to celebrate their first night in their new home with a mountain of chips. For a chef, Laura didn't have a refined palette.

Once home, they curled up on their sofa and ate with music playing in the background.

"I can't believe we're finally here." Laura smiled as she picked up a crispy chip. Could life get any better?

"Nor can I, it's perfect, isn't it?" Sean smiled back at her. It really was.

Before buying the flat they had rented lots of different places, however this was theirs. They could make this place their home for however long they wanted to. The thought filled Laura with joy as she considered all the memories that they would make within these walls.

They had been so happy in that flat, planning their future together. Now all it seemed to hold was bad memories. Laura wasn't sure if she could ever go back there to live.

"You okay?" Greg asked her, sensing that there had been a shift in her mood.

"Just thinking. What do you think our chances are of finding Sean?" Laura wanted to forget about the flat, and the perfect future that she once had planned. That wouldn't be happening now, even if they got out of this alive.

"I'm not sure, Laura. He knows how to go unnoticed. I

think it might be a matter of luck if I'm being brutally honest. We have to try though." Greg was right, they had to try. There was no other option. They had to get to Sean before anyone else could.

The journey seemed to drag as they left the beautiful Welsh scenery behind for the busy city. Greg had arranged for them to stay in a hotel for tonight, then he would try to find out more information from his contacts. Laura hadn't mentioned anything, but she had also been planning to go out wandering the streets, just in case. If it was down to luck, then anything could happen.

Eventually, they arrived in Manchester, this time to a hotel on the outskirts. Laura couldn't help but feel a chill run down her spine. The last time she had been here, Luke had been hoodwinking her. She dearly hoped that she could trust Greg.

Once inside the room, they relaxed a little, Laura put her fears to the back of her mind and they ordered some lunch.

"Shall I put the television on?" Laura asked, settling down after finishing her lunch of soup.

"You can do. I might just give my husband a call if you're okay to entertain yourself for a bit?" Laura nodded in response and tried to avert her attention back to the television. She wondered whether Greg would leave the room to make the phone call. If he did, should she run away? Was she sure she could trust him? Laura didn't know what to think anymore, or who to trust. Before her mind could get too carried away, Greg settled himself down on his bed and made his phone call. Laura instantly relaxed as she heard him chatting away to his husband and asking after their children. It was a relief to know that he hadn't been lying to her.

Laura slowly relaxed on the sofa and tuned into the trashy dating show that was on the television. The sound of Greg on the phone to his husband had become background noise. Her eyelids were growing heavy and she was just about to give in to them when there was a knock on the door. Laura turned to look at Greg, wondering what they should do. He quickly said goodbye and held a finger to his lips, shushing Laura. Slowly, he made his way over towards the door and looked through the peephole.

"Oh, no." He sighed, giving no explanation. Instead, he opened the door and in came four very angry-looking men.

"What the hell are you two playing at?" Jake angrily shouted at them as Greg rapidly shut the door behind them, in case anyone was walking by and heard their conversation.

"It was my fault." Laura stepped forward. She didn't want Greg taking the blame for her crazy plan.

"Yes, it is, but it's also Greg's fault. He should have told us you were planning this. You're lucky the car had a tracker on it so we could follow you." The other men grunted in agreement.

"I'm sorry. Please don't stop me looking for Sean." Laura could feel a sob rising inside of her chest. She was in the same city as Sean again, she couldn't just leave without even trying to find him.

"I won't do that. Laura, I think you ought to sit down." The anger had disappeared from Jake's voice and had been replaced by a kindness that set Laura's nerves on edge.

"Jake, what's going on?" Her voice was shaky as she stepped backwards and sat back down on the sofa. Her legs gave way beneath her.

"We've received information saying that the gang have caught Sean. They've taken him to a warehouse in the area."

Laura had to reach out to grip the side of the sofa to stop herself from blacking out. They had Sean.

"We have to go there." Laura screamed, jumping up from her seat. Nothing would stop her from going to Sean. The gang wanted him and now they had him, it was unlikely they would delay killing him. If she didn't get to him soon, he would be dead.

"We do, but you have to stay here Laura, it's too dangerous." Jake walked towards her, gesturing for her to sit down again. Laura did as she was told, but she held his eye. She would not give in.

"I'm coming with you, Jake. I can help, Sean trained me to shoot. Please." Laura poured every ounce of her emotions into her little speech. Whether or not Jake agreed, she was going. However, it would be easier and safer if she could just tag along with them.

"Let her come. She'll follow us and we cannot afford to leave any officers behind to babysit her." Greg stepped in to argue Laura's case for her. He was right, she would do everything she could to follow them.

"Fine, you can come, but first we need a plan." Jake relented, he knew Laura would be safer with them rather than trying to follow them on her own.

Laura breathed a sigh of relief. Whatever happened next would be the end of all this. Whether it ended with her death, Sean's death or the destruction of the gang, she didn't know.

CHAPTER THIRTY THREE

Laura sat in the back of the car, trying to stop herself from shaking. She was in the car with three of the officers, including Greg and Jake. The plan was that the four of them would enter the warehouse first, leaving the other officers to follow later as a surprise ambush. It was risky. The plan was to use Laura as a distraction, just for long enough for them to get the upper hand. If Sean was still alive, then the gang would want to make him suffer by killing her. Laura was terrified, but she was determined to be brave. They did not know if their plan would work, all they knew was that it was dangerous and there was a good chance they wouldn't survive.

The officers had brought a selection of weapons with them, and Laura was now wearing a bullet-proof vest underneath her oversized hoodie. It was surreal sitting amongst undercover officers, about to be used as bait to save her boyfriend from an organised crime group. Laura hoped she would never have to experience anything like this again. Despite the dangerous situation, Laura's mind was overcome with the realisation that she was the closest she had been to Sean in over a year. In a few short minutes, she would be in the same room as him. Her heartbeat quickened at the thought of being in his arms again. She could only hope that they would make it out of this alive and have a future together.

"You okay?" Greg asked from beside her. His eyes looked sad, and he had been withdrawn for most of the journey.

"No, but I have to do this. Greg, please don't feel as though you have to come with me. None of you have to accompany me. Turn around now and go home to your families." Laura's tone was pleading. As much as she wanted and needed their support, she knew what they were sacrificing. It wasn't fair of her to put them in a situation where they might not see their families again. Laura felt the weight of her actions lie heavy on her shoulders. She was about to take people away from their family by leading them into the mouth of danger. Was it selfish of her to do all of this just to save Sean?

"Laura, we're not just doing this for you. We're saving a fellow officer. We're also stopping an organised crime group who are responsible for many drugs-related deaths and endless corruption and crime. It's why we signed up to the police force and we intend to keep our word and protect civilians." Greg's voice was sincere, he really meant what he was saying.

"When we get out of this alive, I promise to babysit for you so you can take your husband out for dinner." It was good to make plans for after all this. Even if those plans never happened, it gave them hope.

"I'm holding you to that!" Greg beamed back at her and gave her hand a reassuring squeeze.

"Two minutes!" Jake shouted from the driver's seat.

Laura took a deep breath. As soon as they pulled up outside the warehouse, they would jump out of the car and running towards the enemy. They could not delay, surprise would be the only thing on their side.

Those two minutes passed in a blur and soon enough they were pulling up along a road next to the warehouse. One-by-one they jumped out of the car and made the rest of the way on foot. As quietly as possible, they climbed through a gap in the fence and ran towards a backdoor belonging to one of the warehouses. There was nobody guarding it. They wouldn't be expecting anyone to launch a rescue mission for Sean. After all, too many people believed he was just an officer that went rogue. Few knew the truth behind his undercover operation - even Laura didn't think she knew everything.

"You sure you want to do this?" Jake paused before he entered the building and glanced back at Laura. She nodded in response. She didn't trust her voice enough to speak. In truth, her insides were churning, and all she wanted to do was run. However, she couldn't, she had to be brave.

"Stay close, Laura. Any trouble and just shout for one of us. We'll do our best to have your back at all times. If it goes wrong, then leave us and escape." Jake's voice was stern and void of all emotion. He was good at his job. Laura only wished her career as a chef could be of more use to her right now. Being able to cut an onion without crying didn't seem all that impressive in the face of danger.

Laura pushed back the blinding fear as she followed the men into the warehouse - it was bringing back memories of the last time she was in a warehouse like that. For the first week after she had been saved, she had nightmares and every time she closed her eyes she saw Luke lying on the floor, slowly bleeding to death. With every ounce of strength within her, Laura forced her feet to keep moving and to keep up with Jake. Greg was behind her, she knew he would do his best to protect her. Laura also had a gun in her hand, and she knew it was likely that she would need to use it.

The group came to a standstill and Jake pressed a finger to his lips to signal everyone to be quiet. As they stood in the dark hallway, they strained their ears. In the distance there was shouting, lots of shouting. Laura couldn't be sure, but she thought she recognised one voice as Sean's. Courage took a hold of her and she gripped her gun with a new resolve. She would do whatever she had to, to get them out of this alive.

They quickly resumed their tiptoeing along the corridor, they were now walking towards the voices. Decades of rubbish crunched underneath their feet, but thankfully the shouting in the other room masked the noise they were making. As a gunshot sounded, Laura clamped a hand across her mouth to stop herself from screaming. Who had been shot? Every fibre of her being was screaming at her to run towards the danger. She needed to know that Sean was okay.

"We need to hurry," she whispered, forcing everyone to move quicker. After a few seconds of silence, the shouting resumed and Laura was relieved to hear Sean's voice again.

They came to a stop outside a doorway. It looked to lead

into a disused office. The door was shut, but the voices on the other side were clear.

"Where is it?" A man shouted. It was so loud it made Laura jump.

"This is getting boring now. I've told you, I don't know. Now just get on with it and kill me." Sean's voice was calm and collected. The sound made Laura want to kick down the door and run into his arms. She took a deep breath to get her emotions under control. If she didn't, she could get them all killed.

Jake signalled a thumbs up sign to everyone. They all nervously glanced at each other and returned the sign. They were ready to go in. Ready to fight the enemy and to see who would win.

With a deafening blow, Jake kicked down the door and all four of them ran into the room. Laura was surrounded, so she was almost out of sight. Once inside the room, Laura's senses went into overdrive as she took in the scene around her.

She was right; the room had once been an office; it was still filled with desks and chairs. In the middle of the room sat Sean, tied to a revolving chair. He looked completely different to the last time she had seen him. His brown hair was overgrown and was hanging across his eyes so that he had to keep shaking his head to move it to the side. Once she could see his eyes, a pang of sadness reverberated through her. They no longer held that cheeky sparkle, instead they looked tired and withdrawn. His right eye had a huge purple bruise around it and blood was still dripping from his nose. He looked awful, but at the same time he still looked like her Sean. Laura knew that as soon as his arms were around her, he would still feel like her Sean.

"What the hell's going on?" Laura moved her attention from Sean to the man who was shouting. She gasped for breath, feeling as though she had been winded as she inspected the man that stood opposite Sean, holding a gun. It was an older version of Luke. The same dark hair and green eyes. It took a lot of self-control for Laura to stop herself from hyperventilating. Despite Luke's inherently evil nature, a very stupid side of her had started to fall for him. However, being in the same room with Sean again made Laura wonder how she could have ever entertained the thoughts of liking another man. He was her soulmate and nothing would stop her from getting him out of this alive.

"Where are the rest of your men?" Jake shouted. He had noticed the empty room at the same time Laura had. Something was wrong.

"They're dead." Harry spat back at them. His eyes were ablaze with anger.

"All of them?" Greg's voice gave away the shock that he was feeling. Even Laura couldn't quite believe what she was hearing.

"They all betrayed me. They're all dead. You will be, too, in a few minutes.'" Harry's eyes widened as he took in Greg standing opposite him.

"A few minutes?" Jake asked, squaring up next to Greg. It was a look of solidarity, but Laura knew it was also to create a protective wall for her.

"Surely, you boys remember how I like to play with my food? Lull you into a false sense of security." The laugh that escaped Harry's lips sent a chill down Laura's spine. He was truly evil.

"He's just too cowardly to kill you." Sean shouted from behind and Harry whipped around to glare at him. Laura could have killed him herself in that moment. She'd always loved his out-spoken side, but right now it had the potential to get them all killed. His love for living dangerously was something they needed to sit down and talk about.

"You really need to learn to let go." Greg shouted, diverting Harry's attention back to him. Laura could see what they were doing. They were winding Harry up to make him vulnerable to his emotions. However, she suspected that Harry's emotions were not ones to be played with. The anger inside of him would be enough to drag them all down with him. Harry advanced towards Greg.

"Hello, Harry." Greg's voice was filled with anger as he stepped forward slightly. Laura had to move quickly to ensure she was still hidden. However, she saw Sean's face completely change as he spotted her flecks of blonde hair. He knew she was in the room with him and a small smile pulled at the corners of his mouth.

"You've already crossed me once, Gregory. I suggest you leave now, before I kill you."

Harry walked towards them. As his attention was on Greg, Laura took the opportunity to peak around him to see who else was in the room. There was nobody, only Sean sat in the middle. Was Harry being truthful when he said the others were dead? She also wondered what Harry meant when he said that Greg had already crossed him.

"I always knew Luke would grow up to be a disappointment." Greg was shouting now.

"No, Gregory, you're the biggest disappointment. A son who refuses to go into business with his father." Laura had to stop herself from gasping at Harry's words. Did she understand him? Was Greg really his son?

"No, you're the disappointment, dad." Greg snarled back at Harry, his hands forming fists by his sides.

"You were always jealous of Luke. Tell me why I shouldn't put this bullet in your head right now?" His teeth were gritted as he held the gun up, pointing it directly at Greg's head. Laura moved to the right slightly, away from the line of fire. There was a small gap in-between Greg and Jake that she could peer through. Sean's eyes were focused on her, the small sliver that was on show. Unless someone knew she was there, then she would just look like a shadow.

"Yes, so jealous of him." Sarcasm dripped from every word. "So jealous that I killed him."

"Nice try, big brother, but you didn't kill me." Laura gasped as the door opened and in walked Luke. He was alive. Slowly, he advanced on Greg.

"You could never finish a job." Harry snarled at Greg. He lifted the gun and pulled the trigger, however Jake was too quick for him. He pulled Greg out of the way of the firing line, leaving Laura exposed. The bullet just missed her. Harry's face was confused until he realised who she was.

"Laura, how lovely to see you again." A shiver ran down Laura's spine at the sound of Luke's voice. It had once sounded so appealing to her, however, now it filled her with dread and fear. He was a ruthless killer, and she was under no pretences as to how much danger she was in in his presence. Luke continued to move towards Laura as she stood frozen to the spot. She wanted to run but, despite trying, her legs would not move.

"I've missed you." Luke whispered as he stood in front of her and stroked the side of her face.

"Get away from her!" Sean's voice was filled with venom. If they had not tied him to a chair, then Laura knew he would have pulled Luke from her and used him as a punchbag.

"She's never said no to me." Luke's response sparked something inside of Laura. Fury clouded her vision as she clutched the gun by her side.

"You are nothing but a manipulative bully. You fooled me into thinking you cared about me so that you could extract information from me." The gun was heavy in Laura's hand as she held it up and aimed at Luke.

"I'll kill you before you even have a chance to pull that trigger." Harry threatened from the other side of the room, bringing his own gun up to aim at Laura.

A gun shot rung out and Laura jumped, pulling her own trigger. Sean called out her name and Laura felt a sudden pain shoot through her side. She tried to work out what had happened. Luke was staggering backwards, a look of shock on his face before he fell. Blood was seeping out from his chest. Laura fell to the ground as the pain worsened. She had been shot.

"Laura!" Sean cried. He was desperate to go to her, but he was still tied to the chair. Greg ran to her, pulling off his jumper and pressing it against her wound.

"Hey, you're going to be okay. An ambulance is on the way." Laura turned her head to where Harry had been standing. He was lying on the floor in a pool of his own blood.

"Is he dead?" Laura asked, her entire body was shaking. Greg held her hand, whilst Jake went to check Harry's lifeless body. He felt for a pulse and everybody held their breath, waiting for his answer.

"He's dead." Jake announced. He then went over to where Luke was lying, still struggling to hold on to his last ties to life.

"Is anyone going to untie me?" Sean called from his chair. One of the other officers went to his aid whilst their back-up came running into the room.

"What happened?" They asked, looking at the scene in front of them.

"You're a bit late!" Greg's tone was light, he was trying to keep everyone calm.

"Laura!" Sean was finally free, and he was wrapping his arms around her. Greg moved so that Sean could take his place, however he kept nearby so that he could put pressure on her wound.

"I think he's dead." Jake announced as he stood next to Luke. Laura breathed a sigh of relief. Even if she didn't make it, at least Sean would be safe.

"I love you." Sean whispered in her ear. A huge smile spread across Laura's face before her vision went and she passed out in Sean's arms.

CHAPTER THIRTY FOUR

For the second time in her life, Laura woke up in a hospital room with the overly bright artificial lights shining directly into her eyes. She blinked, trying to adjust to the sudden light. As she was trying to adapt to her surroundings, her last memories came flooding back to her. She had just killed somebody, and she had been shot. However, she didn't know what had happened after that. Laura used every ounce of strength that she had left to thwart her overactive brain. Instead, she concentrated on looking around the room. With a sigh of relief, she realised Sean was sitting in the chair next to her bed, softly snoring. A year ago she would have nudged him and got annoyed at his snoring, but having been apart for so long she had almost missed it.

As Sean slept on, Laura enjoyed the moment. He was back beside her, and for now, they were safe. Laura had so many questions that she wanted to ask, but she knew they would keep. Right now, it was time to celebrate their reunion and look towards the future.

"Morning." Sean's voice was gruff from sleep as he rubbed a hand across his face. Laura was grateful that he'd never been able to grow a beard, God only knows how long it would be after a year of no shaving.

"Good morning, sleepyhead." She beamed back at him. It was surreal to be back in his company. Despite a year apart, it was like no time at all had passed. He was still her Sean.

"How are you feeling?" Sean asked. He was more alert now.

"Physically, I feel fine. Well, besides being shot. Mentally, I'm not sure. How about you?" Laura was being honest, she knew it would take a while for her to be completely okay again.

"I'm the same, just some bruising." He reached forward and took hold of her hand. His touch still felt the same, and it still made her heart quicken.

"Sean, what happened?" The question escaped Laura's mouth before she could stop herself. As she heard the words out loud, even she didn't quite know what she meant. Did she mean what happened at the warehouse after she lost consciousness, or did she mean what happened over the past year?

"I think I better start at the beginning, Laura." Sean's face was drawn and his eyes blank. He was carrying the guilt of everything that had happened.

Sean told Laura everything, from how he was assigned to the undercover role, to infiltrating an organised crime group, and stealing drugs from them. His eyes filled with tears as he told her the stories of selling drugs to vulnerable people. He explained that was why he had stolen the drugs so that no more innocent lives would be lost.

"It's okay, Sean, you did the right thing." Laura smiled at him, squeezing his hand to comfort him.

"Oh, Laura, what are we going to do? Our lives are a mess."

Laura pulled back the bedsheet and gestured for him to climb in besides her. He did as he was asked and as soon as he was next to her she was in his arms.

"It's going to be okay," she whispered, enjoying the feeling of being in his embrace. "Sean, what happened in the warehouse after I blacked out? Am I in trouble for killing someone?" The questions had been gnawing away at Laura since the second she regained consciousness, and she couldn't keep them at bay any longer.

"You're not in any trouble, I promise you. It was self defence and you have police officers as witnesses." Sean paused for a moment to allow the news to sink in, Laura immediately relaxed.

"Actually, you're a bit of a hero. You helped bring down one of the most dangerous gang leaders in the north." Sean let out a bemused chuckle as he told her, and Laura couldn't help but giggle. Perhaps she could do slightly more than cut up an onion without crying.

"You taught me well. So what happened?" Laura was impatient to hear what had happened whilst she was unconscious.

"We ran, well I carried you. We were worried that Harry might have had a few gang members lurking around, so instead of waiting for the ambulance, we jumped in the cars, drove you to the hospital and called the police on the way."

"And then what?" Laura wanted to know everything she could.

"You were admitted to hospital. They said you were lucky to be alive. The bullet just missed any internal organs. The police then came and took statements from everyone and confirmed that Harry and Luke are dead. They'll want to speak to you at some point too, but we're all okay and nobody is in trouble." Sean finished his explanation with a kiss, preventing Laura from asking anymore questions. Even after a year apart, he still knew her so well. Knowing how close to death she had been made her want to treasure every second that she had with Sean. She had finally found him.

They laid in silence for a while, enjoying each other's company and knowing that the worst was over. What would happen next, neither of them knew, but for now they were together and that was all that mattered.

The police took a statement from Laura and reassured her she wouldn't be facing prosecution for shooting Luke. For the time being, it was decided that she and Sean would be safer at the hospital with a guard stationed at the door. The police were almost certain that they had arrested the last of the gang members, but they wanted to be safe. Decisions would need to be made as to what happened next. Witness protection was mentioned, but everyone was reluctant to make that decision. For now, they would be safe with armed officers protecting them. Laura and Sean were in the middle of discussing their options when there was a knock at the door. To their relief, in poured their immediate family. It was a tight squeeze to fit everyone in the room, but that was instantly forgotten about as they were enveloped in hugs and kisses. It had been an awful year, but it had finally ended.

EPILOGUE

25th October 2021

"Are you ready for another day?" Sean asked. He walked towards the door and pulled back the heavy brass bolt.

"Let them in!" Laura called from her place behind the bar. They were running late today, and she was still wiping the sticky surface left over from yesterday. As she moved an old newspaper, she glanced down and was shocked to see that it was almost two years since Sean's disappearance.

So much had changed since, and her life was now unrecognisable. After Laura had shot Harry, they had spent three days in hospital before being moved to a cottage in a quaint Welsh village. They then spent a few months there, both receiving therapy to help them process everything they had witnessed. The police had thanked Sean, both physically and financially, for his help, and had let him go. However much he would have liked to continue to serve as an officer, it was impossible. Slowly, they had pieced themselves back together and their relationship had grown even stronger.

Two months after the move to Wales, their flat in Manchester sold, and they had to make a more permanent decision for their future. Eventually, they had stumbled across a village pub that was within their budget. After viewing it, they had immediately fallen in love with the quaint building and the local punters. Laura and Sean were now the proud owners of The Beehive Inn - a homage to their Manchester roots. Laura spent her days using her skills and cooking for their customers. Meanwhile, Sean charmed everyone at the bar, and when it came to closing time, he would use his experience as a police officer to throw out their rowdy customers.

"Morning!" One of their regular customers, Charles, called as he came through the doors. It was a Saturday morning and by midday the pub would be heaving with people. Laura's food kept the locals coming back for more. Sean liked to think it was his personality and witty banter, but Laura knew better.

"Usual?" Sean called as he joined Laura behind the bar.

"Yes, please. You're Sean Scott, aren't you?" Charles asked, squinting over the bar.

"Yes." Sean replied. He had frozen with a glass in his hand. They didn't make a point of making their full names known.

"You're in the paper!" Charles exclaimed as he handed Laura the day's paper.

With trembling hands, Laura unfolded the paper and glanced at the front page. Her heart hammered in her chest as she saw the heading; 'Drug gang jailed for 20 years'.

"Sean," she whispered, turning the paper so that he could read the heading.

Laura skimmed the writing to see that her and Sean's names were mentioned as witnesses in the case. Thankfully, the police believed they had tracked down all the members of the gang that were still alive. Laura had forgotten that their sentencing was due. Relief flooded her body as she realised that the remaining members were now in prison. Their nightmare was finally over.

"Charles, can I offer you a pie on the house in exchange for not pointing this out to anyone?" Laura smiled sweetly over the bar at the elderly man. The last thing they needed was for their regulars to be gossiping about their past.

"Throw in my ale and you've got yourself a deal!" He chuckled, taking the paper back from Laura and immediately flicking to the sports pages.

"You okay?" Laura moved closer to where Sean stood, still frozen to the spot with a glass in hand.

"Yeah. Just a bit of a shock." Sean tried to smile, but Laura wasn't fooled. After everything that had happened, Sean had found it difficult to process it all. He still woke throughout the night with vivid nightmares.

"It's over. Now we can really start to re-build our lives." Laura reached up on her tiptoes to plant a kiss on his lips.

"I love you." He smiled at her, snapping out of the initial shock.

"I love you too. I better get Charles his pie." With a final glance back at Sean, Laura made her way into the kitchen. It would take some time for Sean to heal from everything he had been through, but they would be okay

- they had found each other.

About Elizabeth Holland

Elizabeth Holland is a keen writer of romance novels. She enjoys the escapism of picking up a book and transporting yourself into a new world. With her mind bursting with lots of different stories Elizabeth is exploring the world of self-publishing her novels.

You can contact Elizabeth on Twitter @EHollandAuthor

Thank you for reading.
I would greatly appreciate it if you could take the time to leave a review on Amazon and/or Goodreads.

Other books by Elizabeth Holland

The Vintage Bookshop of Memories

"Nothing but our happiness should dictate what we do with our lives"

Prue Clemonte loves history. When Prue returns to Ivy Hatch after her grandmother's death she has no idea just how much the village's history is about to change her life. With endless secrets and ancient feuds Prue must uncover memories to discover the village's history.

As Prue inherits *The Vintage Bookshop of Memories* she discovers a diary which details her mother's thoughts, memories and secrets. The shop is like stepping into her mother's mind and Prue is determined to restore the shop. However, with a village full of people against her can Prue win them over and honour her mother's memory, whilst trying to discover the truth about the past?

Prue won't let a village full of people who hate her stop her from living her life and being happy. With the help of Elliot Harrington Prue is determined to win the village over and make herself a life back home in Ivy Hatch. However, she soon begins to realise that she's lost herself in her quest for the truth. As Prue battles to find herself can she save the bookshop, whilst also stopping the village from ruining her life? There's also Elliot Harrington, handsome and perfect and yet their relationship is doomed from the start.

Christmas at The Vintage Bookshop of Memories

Whisk yourself away to the village of Ivy Hatch and enjoy the Christmas Day celebrations...

Katie Wooster's life has been turned upside down; she's single, homeless and unemployed. With Christmas around the corner, Katie finds herself in *The Vintage Bookshop of Memories.* As the village's magical charm begins to weave its way into Katie's heart, can her best friend, Prue Clemonte, persuade her to leave the past behind her and open her heart to romance again? Local farmer, Austin Harrington is ready to sweep her off of her feet, but Katie isn't sure she's ready for a new relationship.

As Katie watches her best friend marry her soulmate, she wonders whether she can have her own *happily ever after.*

Return to Ivy Hatch this Christmas, where the residents are waiting to celebrate with you...

The Balance Between Life and Death

The balance between life and death can be precarious. Ana Adams wakes up every morning, goes to work and comes home at night to her dog. That doesn't mean she's living. After suffering the worst pain imaginable Ana is trying to make it through each day. The smile on her face means nothing, all that matters is the turmoil that is going on inside her head.

As Ana learns to open up to others and embarks on a new relationship she finds that letting life in is harder than she anticipated. Perhaps she's moved too fast and needs to focus on healing before opening herself up to more pain and disappointment.

Will Ana learn her lesson or will it be too late for her?

This novella focuses on the importance of putting your mental health first.
A reminder that you never know what someone is hiding beneath their smile.

Printed in Great Britain
by Amazon

57492178R10129